ARGENT

Argent — The Unicorn (Book One)

Finalist Winner — Fantasy

2025 Hollywood Book Festival

"Fantasy lovers, immerse yourself in RK Jack's enthralling action-adventure novella, Argent. When young Darrow invites eighteen-year-old Graciela (Grace) for an adventure in the Hallowdale Forest, little does she imagine that they will inadvertently wake up an ancient evil buried in the forbidden Amorak Cemetery …

Filled to the brim with suspense and action, Argent is a gripping fantasy novella with magic, mystery, and lore galore. As a fantasy fan, I absolutely loved this book. Author RK Jack doesn't waste a word and delivers a concisely crafted narrative with a fast-paced plot that has you on the edge of your seat from start to finish. From the very first pages, you feel the stakes as you're not sure if your favorite characters will make it out alive by the end. Argent steals every scene she is in, but I also enjoyed the secondary characters like Grace, Clestus, Drek, and Shivalt. The author has built an immersive fantasy world that is easy to get lost in. The action sequences are thrilling, and you don't want to put the book down in the middle of a battle. Fantasy readers will love this."

NIGHTMARE

ARGENT — THE UNICORN

BOOK TWO

RK JACK

CONTENTS

NIGHTMARE

Published by Horizon View Press LLC

Denver, CO

ISBNs:

Print—Paperback: 979-8-9900568-8-6

Print—Hardcover: 978-1-968210-01-4

Ebook: 978-1-968210-00-7

LCCN: 2025921336

BISAC: FIC009120 **FICTION** / Fantasy / Dragons and Mythical Creatures

First Edition: November 2025

Cover and Interior Design by: Horizon View Press.

Copyright owned by Russell Jack (RK Jack).

Publisher's Cataloging-in-Publication Data:

Publisher's Cataloging-in-Publication Data

Names: Jack, Russell Keith, author.

Title: Nightmare / R.K. Jack.

Series: Argent—The Unicorn

Description: Denver, CO: Horizon View Press LLC, 2025.

Identifiers: LCCN: 2025921336 | ISBN: 978-1-968210-01-4
(hardcover) | 979-8-9900568-8-6 (paperback) | 978-1-968210-00-7
(ebook)

Subjects: LCSH Unicorns--Fiction. | Shapeshifters--Fiction. |
Shapeshifting--Fiction. | Fantasy fiction. | BISAC FICTION / Fantasy
/ Dragons and Mythical Creatures

Classification: LCC PS3610 .A35 N54 2025 | DDC 813.6--dc23

PART I

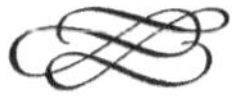

THE NIGHTMARE RISES

CHAPTER 1

DARK WIZARD KILROG

The moon was at its apex; it was now or never. Only when the moon is at its strongest could the spell work. I was summoning a demon, a mount worthy of my excellent skills as a dark wizard.

I had not yet attained the secrets of immortal life, but I had a destination in mind that would give it to me. First, I needed a steed and companion that could help me in my desire to spread evil throughout the land.

A *nightmare*.

The arcane spell took untold years and a small fortune to procure, but I had done it. The creature that would arise from ash and fire was a thing of terrifying beauty. With a body of the purest black and eyes, hooves, and mane of fire, it would be critical in my desire for eternal life.

The trek through the bog was treacherous, but I had arrived at where the ancient pedestal once stood.

Using powerful spells, I peeled away the muck and weeds until the ancient dark opalus talisman stood before me.

"At last," I said aloud.

Putting out my wards, which are protective spells, I also made a *Force Dome* to keep any creatures or weather of the wetlands from disturbing me.

Over the following days, I chanted and used the components for the summoning spell. Everything had to be perfect, or it would be for nothing. As the moon had waxed to full and was just beginning to wane, the spell was done.

All was still.

Everything around sensed that something unnatural was happening.

HISSSSS …

The ground split open, and a dark mist came out. The mist was an inky black, with tendrils in it that moved as though alive. It smelled of brimstone and sulfur, but there was no fire. This was disconcerting; there was supposed to be fire …

CRACK!

The ground in front of the pedestal ruptured completely, and I saw a giant warhorse of the darkest blackness of the abyss emerge. Its eyes shone, not of fire, but of a silver to rival the glow of the moon. An unnatural darkness poured from its body. It locked eyes with me, and I could feel its telepathic contact. So, I allowed it in—

Why have you summoned me?

Her voice, telepathically speaking into my mind, was alluring and terrifying at the same time.

"I am powerful, but I need allies if I am to achieve my goals," I said aloud.

Hmm ... And what might those goals be?

"There is a dungeon that holds the key to eternal life, but I need a steed that can carry me through the Bog of the Dead. Only a nightmare can do this. First, however, there is a signet I must procure to find it ..."

She looked at me in silence, contemplating my words before finally speaking again.

Are you evil?

"Yes."

Then I will aid you, as long as I see fit.

Beyond the now-disappearing *Force Dome*, I could see the marsh's wisps of mist rising in the moonlight. I glanced down and saw that all the vegetation near the nightmare was wilting and unhealthy. The creature, the demon before me, was not what I had expected. The utter blackness of the steed was almost unnatural, like all light was sucked in, never to return. A surprise, as this was not a nightmare I had ever heard of.

You are questioning what I am? Good. Your spell worked better than you know—

I heard a rustling and saw a crocodile wading up out of the bog toward us. It was huge and clearly hungry.

Suddenly it stopped.

There was a strange, crackling sound coming from inside it, and it was now completely still as it took on a peculiar, greyish sheen.

I looked back at the iridescent silver eyes of this demon. They were fixated on the now fully petrified crocodile.

"Impressive" was all I could muster.

What in God's name had I summoned?

She clearly understood my thoughts. Laughing in my head, I heard her response.

It was not in God's name; right idea, but wrong direction. My name is Onyx. I am a greater demon and the Queen of all Nightmares. I am the one and only death-mare from the planes of hell.

She bent her knees and allowed me to sit astride her. Standing again, we began the long walk toward our destination.

The marsh eventually opened to a forest, but I missed the transition. The long hours of the spell had depleted me, and I awoke to the first rays of dawn filtering through the high tree canopy above. It was cold, but I had maintained a *Warmth* spell before dozing off. I warmed up quickly after casting it again, although I didn't feel well-rested. If the cold bothered my steed, it did not show. A warm late spring day beckoned. For now, though, the night was still cold.

Stretching, I looked around. Something was amiss. Critically, I scanned my environment.

The trees and everything around us looked normal, but I heard no wildlife nearby. There were sounds in the distance, but never near us. Looking around, I gasped.

Behind us was a faint trail, barely noticeable in the

darkness unless you looked closely, but I could see a five-meter-wide path of wilting plants and small animals dead along it. I also noticed, for the first time since being in the swamp, that no insects were near me either.

Well, that is a boon.

It seems that life is an anathema to this creature. If not for my usefulness to it, I am sure it would have killed me straight away.

Or at least tried, as I have many robust defenses I can employ.

I felt bone-weary tired, so I nodded off again ...

* * *

ONYX—QUEEN OF THE NIGHTMARES

I FELT the mage fall asleep astride me. He was exhausted from the ordeal of summoning me, which was no small feat. However, I knew he was also being drained of his life force. If I had wished it, I could have drained much, much more. This human wizard had me intrigued, though. I would enjoy seeing how much evil he could commit. At the first sign of squeamishness or a guilty conscience, I would end him.

Soon, I would know if he was truly evil or not.

I knew he must have had a *Ring of Regeneration,* or else my slow life drain would have killed him from contact with me. Not surprising for a powerful wizard to have such an item.

As I cleared the edge of the forest, a small walled town stood across the field from me. I knew my current form would not engender me to its inhabitants. Not that I cared, but I enjoy a little fun before just killing the good townfolk. So, coming in as a humanoid was a better bet.

At least I hope so, as I do enjoy playing with my foes before slaying them. I thought about the many different humanoids on Yrth we would soon encounter …

There are the elves, dexterous and clever from their many years of life and combat. They generally have great magic items to aid them, and many have elven chainmail — a lighter and stronger version that only elves can make. Not even the mighty dwarves know how to make it. Ah, yes, the dwarves. Shorter than humans but muscular and stubborn. They made excellent warriors and blacksmiths; some are even wise in the ways of engineering. The halflings, well, they are pretty much useless except for their knack with traps and small spaces.

BOOM

With a loud rumble that sounded like low thunder, an opaque black cloud of miasma erupted where I stood. As it cleared, I was now visible as a human.

Well, mostly anyway.

I knew a black-skinned human should not stand out too much; they would just assume I was a Drow, a form of elf that is usually evil or at least apathetic to the feelings of others. A closer look would reveal I was no

Drow; my ears were those of a normal human. My studded leather helm hid that particular feature.

We cleared the tree line at a leisurely pace and crossed the meadow to the walled town in the distance. As expected, we were hailed as soon as we drew near the town's main gate.

"Halt! Who goes there?"

A large man in plate mail and chain had approached us as we neared the gate. He had several soldiers with him.

"I am Onyx, and this is my companion, Archmage Kilrog. We seek food and supplies within your town."

The man looked at me and was clearly suspicious of me, of us. His eyes narrowed, and he scowled. I could feel that this man was a creature of good. Not all of the other soldiers were, as I sensed one that was truly evil.

Casually, I glanced at him, and he subtly nodded to me. Good, he felt it as well.

After several moments that seemed to stretch on forever, the man leading them finally spoke.

"Very well. I am Captain Theodus. Welcome to Greenlove Village. It is me you will see again if you misbehave, however, so be sure to be on your best behaviour in my town."

With that, he and the other soldiers turned back to the main gate, which was now slowly opening.

Smiling a cold smile, I followed them inside. Above, I could see the raised portcullis and the murder holes—where boiling oil could be poured and even ignited to stop intruders, or other nasty things tossed down on them.

The smell of livestock, cooking food, and a whiff of excrement greeted me.

Ah, it's good to be in a town again.

Several townsfolk stopped what they were doing and stared. Each, in turn, looked away as I glared at them.

I knew I was a striking sight.

It was not just my inky black skin, but also my wild, waist-length raven black hair and pale silver eyes. The fact that I was as tall and muscular as a large man was also noticeable. Standing a full eighteen hands and weighing an incredibly lean and muscular fifteen stone, I was extremely intimidating. My all-black studded leather armor and great sword only added to my ferocity. The looks I gave did not help. My cruelty and malice were constantly reflected in my eyes and vicious smile.

The wizard next to me also did not disguise his moral alignment. With dark black and purple robes and skulls and body parts in various bags hanging from his tunic and belt, it was clear he was a necromancer, among other classes of spells.

People in town gave us a wide berth as we headed to the local drinking hole.

As we entered the One-Eyed Lemur, the tables fell silent one by one. Casually, I scanned the room. Many good people, as well as some of a more neutral or lawful-neutral disposition, looked my way.

Pity.

I was hoping to find at least one of them radiating evil. Guess I will just have to find that one guard again.

"May I help ye, miss … ?"

I turned my attention to the barkeep. She was an older woman with red hair just starting to go grey. She had an ample bosom and wore only a simple shopkeeper's outfit.

"Aye, my name is Onyx, and this is my companion, Archmage Kilrog, and we are seeking strong companions for a dangerous quest. However, I see nothing of interest in here."

Several men looked angered by my comment, but wisely kept to their drinks and tables.

"Welp, I can't be helpin' with that, my lady. Perhaps a drink?"

She smiled a practiced smile, but I could feel her discomfort. Several bar patrons were also on edge, an effect of my aura of evil.

"Yes. The blood of a maiden virgin, please."

The barkeep blanched as I chuckled.

"Never mind, just a pint of ale for us each then."

Without another word, Kilrog and I took a corner table. No one could get behind us, and we could see the whole of the room. Several eyed us with contempt or worry, or both —

SWOOSH

The pub door opened to a gust of wind, and three soldiers entered. One was the evil one that I saw outside the gate. He looked around the room and finally spied me. He smiled at me, and I returned the gesture. His cadre of soldiers walked straight to my table.

Kilrog and I did not bother to stand.

As he stood before me, he just stared lasciviously at me, eyeing me up and down with a smirk. Strangely, he did not seem to be intimidated or turned off by the fact that I was as big and strong as he was.

This is not entirely true, of course.

As a deathmare, I possessed the strength of the most muscular warhorse you could find, one weighing over a hundred stone, even in my human form. I could easily toss him across the room if I wished.

Instead, I smiled at his evil behaviour. He would make an excellent sellsword if I could entice him to join us.

"Enjoying the view?" I asked.

"Aye, indeed, very much so. But that is not why I am here."

"Well then, please do enlighten us."

He looked at me for another moment, staring straight at my breasts, then looked up into my eyes.

"My Captain, whom you have meet, wants us to keep an eye on you. So I shall ..." He smirked as he said it.

I truly appreciated his blatant disregard for my dignity. His evil was invigorating.

It was almost as if he could hear what I was thinking, so I reached out into his mind ... and he let me in.

Hail, fine dark elf. What truly brings you here?

I am seeking companions for a dangerous quest. You appear to have the right temperament, one of duplicity and evil. Are you intrigued?

Yes, yes! My name is Sergeant Telisgard. What do I need to do to join you?

I glanced about the room and found one man staring at me with a contemptuous gaze.

"See that man over there?" I said aloud, pointing.

Telisgard turned and looked, then also said aloud, "Yes, I see him."

"He fondled me without permission, and I want him arrested!" I said.

The man paled and looked around helplessly.

Yes, I am enjoying his torment and confusion!

"I did no such thing! She is evil and just causing trouble!" he yelled.

Several patrons nodded in agreement and stood up.

"By order of the guard, you are under arrest! The rest of you, stay seated!" Telisgard yelled.

Smirking, I watched the spectacle.

Everyone in the pub knew the man was innocent, but Telisgard was the sergeant, so they were making an arrest regardless. I could feel the other two having reservations; they would bear watching ...

Several patrons sat back down, but others did not.

"Do not interfere—"

WHAP!

The first man to stand ran forward and tackled my newfound sellsword guard. The other two were quickly overrun as well. The rest of the room felt emboldened and joined in the melee.

The townspeople knew something was amiss, but they also knew that killing the guards would result in their hanging. So, it was fists and feet. The guards put up a hell of a fight, but numbers matter, and they were losing.

With a sigh, I glanced at Kilrog and nodded.

He stood and stretched out both hands. Lightning crackled and filled the room.

Men started screaming as electricity knocked them off their feet. One took out a wickedly long dagger and charged Kilrog.

THWAP

The electricity stopped, and no one moved.

THUMP

In the sudden quiet, all could hear the man's head as it fell onto the wooden floor of the pub.

My *Vorpal Greatsword* of *the Leech* was held in both hands before me, its jet-black blade pulsed with blood-red for a moment and then returned to its original deep black color. I could feel its *Absorb Health* effect, even though I was uninjured. Everyone was dead quiet, and we could all hear the blood from the strike making a drip, drip, drip sound in the sudden silence …

"What have you done?" asked one of the three guards.

This one was not like the other two. He was neutral in alignment, and my action was not acceptable to him.

I could sense there was some good in him after all. I knew he would no longer work for me, so—

My eyes grew in intensity to a glowing silver, and he stiffened up. All were watching aghast; no one moved.

In my peripheral vision, I could see that Telisgard was smiling evilly through his swollen jaw.

As the guard who dared to backtalk me finished turning to stone, I addressed the crowd.

"We will be leaving now. *Please*, stand in our way, I would *really* enjoy it ..."

As I sheathed my greatsword on my back, the two remaining guards and I strode past the now fully armed men. I deliberately passed close to one on the way out.

As I had hoped, he played the hero.

If I had normal reflexes, he would have had me.

He lunged in surprisingly fast with his shortsword, no doubt aided by adrenaline. I casually side-stepped it and threw a round kick into his chest. He flew back with a sickening crack. I knew the wounds were grievous and probably lethal, so I started laughing.

Still chuckling, we left the bar with our two newest companions.

We had just walked out of the town gates when I heard a phalanx of armed guards approaching behind us. Turning, I saw that the Captain was with them, and he spoke.

"Halt! You are under arrest!" he bellowed.

Smiling, I waved back over my head as I turned and walked away. Before they could mount an attack, Kilrog cast a spell—*Spark Storm*.

The sky darkened, and lightning flashed down. Typically, this spell takes a while to form. However, between his *Ring of Weather Control* and his insanely high skill with the magic, it happened in a mere second or two.

One guard was knocked off his feet and fell to the ground, smoking. Dozens more flashes came down, as the area behind us turned into an electrical lightning attack. The remaining guards quickly retreated inside the town walls.

As I walked away, I could hear the anguished cries of the guards still echoing in my head.

Glorious.

We were now a party of four as we headed down the road toward the next town.

Hmm, I still needed more sellswords ...

CHAPTER 2

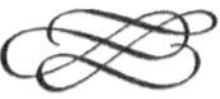

ARGENT THE UNICORN

*D*rinking from a fresh stream, I could see my reflection.

A white horse with a golden horn and blue eyes looked back at me. I was the size of a big horse, strong, lean, and muscular, with golden hooves and a silver mane. Standing a full seventeen hands at the withers and eighty-five stone in weight, I knew I was both a beautiful and intimidating sight.

I lifted my head in alarm.

Something was wrong.

At first, I didn't even see it, but then I looked closer.

The grass and undergrowth near me formed a visible trail through my forest. A five-meter-wide path of wilting plants, along with dead insects and small animals, indicated the direction of travel — it continued in the direction of Greenlove Village.

The winter had come and passed unremarkably, and

spring was fully here, showing in the budding plants and some perennial flowers beginning to emerge here and there. It was midday and comfortably warm as I started following the path. Even some tree limbs above had wilted at whatever had passed through.

What could cause such a life-drain?

It was a conundrum.

I knew of many creatures in this land, and none could cause such an effect.

Since this was my home, I had to know what had caused this.

As a unicorn, I had taken to identifying with and protecting this forest, Hallowdale Forest, as my home, and it has been so for over a century.

The nearby town had recently survived an attack by a powerful necromancer, a lich named Vzerie. With my help and the help of a war party, we found its lair and defeated it, saving the town from its undead horde. As always, there was a price to be paid—not just the large section of forest that the lich had burned, but the lives lost in stopping it.

Including the members of our party who were lost, along with those who succumbed to their wounds from the battle at the town, we had lost over a hundred people to this atrocity. Most of the original war party had stayed in the village, with only the dwarf, Drek the Stout, moving on.

FLASH

As I approached the edge of the tree line, I shifted from a unicorn into a human. A bright flash of sunlight always marks this transformation, one of the many magical effects of being a unicorn.

Now I appeared as a beautiful twenty-year-old woman, with long silver hair and mesmerizing blue eyes. I stood at seventeen hands and weighed but eleven stone. I did not look exceptionally dangerous.

But I was.

I still had the strength of a unicorn, even as a person —that, and over a hundred years of training and experience. So, it was a deceiving look.

My equipment and items changed with me from a unicorn to a human, and disappeared when I changed back. It is an innate magic that still befuddles the best mages today. I was now wearing my magical arms and armor: white leather armor, *Bracers of Defense*, a *Vorpal Shortsword*, a *Longbow of Accuracy*, and a *Cornucopia of Arrows*.

I also carried a magic dagger, sling, and *fire-stones* from our late thief, Toad. A *Xorn* had killed him in the lich's dungeon.

If we ever had to form a war party again, a thief for our party would be a top priority. Although most of them were not great fighters, Toad's trap skills had saved all of our lives multiple times. He was a good man and will be sorely missed.

The wind was blowing gently, and I could still smell the pine trees as I started across the clearing towards the town. Soon, a town guard on the wall saw me and waved.

The gates slowly opened as I approached.

Greenlove Village's townsfolk all knew about me and my true nature, but were sworn to secrecy from outsiders.

There's a small fortune to be made from selling a unicorn's hooves and horn. They hold incredible amounts of mana, a great boon to any magical construct.

Mana is what mages use to cast spells and create magical items. It exists as a life force surrounding us, particularly in the health and fatigue of animals. However, it can be magically concentrated into *power-stones*. Mages rely on these instead of fatigue and health to cast spells, making them very valuable. The mana from unicorn parts will significantly enhance this process. Therefore, the secret is vital for a unicorn, unless you want to become a target for poachers.

"Hail, Lady Argent!"

I waved to the soldier and smiled. I didn't know his name, but I knew his face from my time battling against the undead, shoulder to shoulder with him and the other guards.

Walking in, I was warmly greeted by the townspeople.

"G'day, me Lady!" and "Argent! So good to see you!" greeted me as I made my way to the One-Eyed Lemur —the only pub in town and a great place to pick up news and goings-on. Arriving at the pub, I entered the dusty, sun-lit main room.

"Argent, Bless me!"

Gretchen came over and hugged me fiercely.

"Hi, Gretchen. How's the pub?"

Her smile darkened and fell.

"We had a bit of a dust-up, I'm afraid," she said.

I looked past her.

There was a small contingent of town guards, and I recognized Captain Theodus amongst them. He saw me and nodded my way.

I could also see a lot of blood on the floor, still being cleaned up.

"I am sorry to hear that. Can you tell me more?"

"Just what I told the Captain. A black-skinned woman, a drow by the name of Onyx, came in with a mage by her side. His name was Archmage Kilrog. She was as big as a man and was the most evil person I have ever met. She accused Greg of molesting her, which was false. We had watched her since she entered, and no one had touched her …"

Gretchen paused before continuing, her tale clearly a fresh trauma.

"Three town guards had come in looking for her, and one of them, Sergeant Telisgard, ordered Greg arrested. The townsfolk fought back without using weapons. At that point, the mage cast *Chain Lightning* on the whole room. Then, this woman, this *drow*—" she said distastefully, "she cut off Steve's head. That is when things went downhill. Another man, Erignor, went to stab her with his sword, and she kicked him so hard that it crushed his ribcage and threw him several meters back. How could she kick that hard? He died shortly after …"

Gretchen looked a bit pale, but I had to know more. She saw my look, and I placed a hand on her shoulder.

She reached up and held it.

"So, then one of the three guards protested, and she turned him to stone. Oh, Argent, it was horrible—her eyes glowed silver, and Roland turned into a statue. We had done nothing to her! Why was she so evil?"

I could see tears forming in her eyes.

Gretchen was a sweet woman and had seen a lot in her years as a pub owner and barkeep. This was clearly something truly terrifying.

"She and the mage left the bar. The Captain and guards tried to stop her when she got to the gates, but the mage cast some sort of lightning weather spell, driving the guards back inside the walls. Argent, you could feel the coldness of death when she was near you; I don't know how else to describe it ..."

I removed my hand and nodded, then hugged her.

"I will get to the bottom of it, Gretchen," I promised her, speaking softly in her ear.

As I broke our embrace, Captain Theodus stopped what he was doing and walked over to us.

"Argent, I am glad you are here. The two strangers apparently recruited a couple of my former guards and left town this morning. They were headed toward Hammersfeld, as far as we last saw them. My guess is she is building up an army of sellswords for something. All I know is she turned two of my guards to her employ, killed two townspeople, and turned one of my guardsmen, Roland, to stone. Luckily, between Mayor

Clestus's *Stone to Flesh* spell and the apothecary, he is expected to recover fully …"

He trailed off and clearly was expecting me to say something.

"As I said to Gretchen, I will help you find this woman and her party and stop them. She is clearly an evil woman."

Nodding, he spoke again, "I know you will. There is a small group, a full squad, of town guards I ordered to accompany you; they will meet you at the town gate."

With that, he turned and resumed interviewing the patrons. I watched him go; he was a good man.

"Argent! Well, blessed by Herates we are indeed!"

As I turned toward the door, I happily saw Mayor Clestus—also known as Mage Clestus—Shivalt the Elf, and Lieutenant Graciela walking into the room. They were dressed in full adventuring gear, so I knew they had been summoned after the attack.

As soon as Grace saw me, she squealed in delight and ran into my arms.

"Argent! We have missed you!"

She kissed my cheek, and I smiled warmly. Shivalt came over and hugged me, also.

Graciela, or just Grace to her friends, and Shivalt had been an item ever since we finished fighting the lich. Both of them were fine warriors, and Grace had recently been promoted to the rank of Lieutenant of the Guard.

"We just heard of the commotion at the pub, still getting the details—" Grace started to say.

"They are not far ahead of us, heading towards Hammersfeld. I have their names and details. Care to join me in the hunt?"

They both smiled; it did not even have to be asked. They looked to Theodus, who had heard me, then to Clestus, and they both nodded yes.

"Alright then, let's go. I will brief you all on what Gretchen and Theodus told me on the way…"

I could see that Grace was wearing the chain and splint mail of a town guard, along with her magical shortsword and longbow.

Next to her, Shivalt had his usual assortment of magic: jewelry, a bastard sword, and a longbow. He also wore magical elven chainmail and *Boots of Dexterity*. Attached to his belt was the *Net of Ensnarement*. In addition to his naturally high dexterity and his boots, he was also an expert with sword and bow, as well as throwing that net.

As for Mage Clestus, he had his *Staff of Immolation*, grey robes, a strange wizard's hat, and various items and magical jewelry as found on a successful mage. Like me, he also carried several *power-stones*.

We headed from the pub and out to the town gate. As the four of us walked to the gate, I started repeating everything I knew of our new foes …

* * *

ONYX—QUEEN OF THE NIGHTMARES

THE DIRT ROAD WAS WELL-MAINTAINED, clearly for the benefit of the horse-drawn carriages. As we slogged along the dusty and dung-covered road, I smiled at our good fortune.

I was still in human form, so as not to draw even more attention to our party. Having found two new sellswords, professional town guards no less, we were well on our way to forming a group for our quest.

Kilrog had told me of our final destination and its secret.

The townfolk of Greenlove had defeated the Lich Vzerie and looted its lair, but they were not aware of the value of a small coin-like signet. All of the items from the lich and its abode were sold in the nearby city of Hammersfeld. No one there even knew of the crown, only of the jewels, gold, and other strange items that came from the battle.

We were after only one thing—that signet. Looking like a small copper coin, it displayed the runes of a long-lost language. To the average, or even well-versed, historian, it would appear to be nothing but jibberish. But in the ancient form of Eldritch Evil language that he and I knew, it would unlock the doors to where the lich found the secrets to eternal unlife. All we had to do was find it.

As we walked, we got many strange looks. Several street vendors tried to sell us food or equipment, but we ignored them all. Finally, I found a merchant who sold jewelry and other delicate items.

"Hail, glorious adventurers. How may I aid and equip thee?"

The man was short and quite fat—an unattractive fellow with a greasy face and an even greasier smile.

"Just browsing," I said.

Kilrog and I were looking through his wares. He had a couple of magic items, gold, jewelry, and gems, but also some of the arcane items that once belonged to the lich. Amongst them, next to a tiny ruby, I saw the signet coin. So, I picked up the small ruby gem next to it.

"How much for this little gem?"

"One platinum piece and she'll be yours, beautiful lady!" He smiled as he beamed at me.

I pondered for a bit. The gem was useless to me, but I had a plan in mind.

"Hmm. Seems a bit much, I was thinking more like a single gold …"

He frowned.

"Four gold."

I deliberately let myself look conflicted, but acted like I had just seen the signet for the first time.

"What the hell is that?" I pointed at the signet.

"Oh, that? Just some weird, random coin …"

He got a mischievous look on his face.

"Tell ya what, make it a platinum and I will throw it in for free!"

"No. But I will give you the four gold, if you throw in the coin for free."

"Sold! To the mysterious woman with fine taste!"

He handed me the ruby and the signet, and I gave him four gold coins in return.

Kilrog looked at me in wonder as we walked out of earshot.

"What an idiot. He clearly didn't know what he had," Kilrog said.

I smiled and nodded.

Now we could concentrate on finding a thief and another fighter or two. After all, Hammersfeld was a decent-sized city; there would be plenty of sellswords looking for work.

DARK WIZARD KILROG

I already knew of the tale of the lich, Vzerie, that had been slain at the last town. Its lair, the mausoleum in the center of Amorak Cemetery, was raided and looted by the townspeople, leaving nothing of value behind. Its crown had been melted down, and the gold and jewels sold off. It made a hefty sum for the town's coffers, not to mention the notoriety the town got when word of the tale got out.

We couldn't care less about any of that, but the crown being from a lich caught my attention.

Unbeknownst to the dimwitted townsfolk, the only truly valuable item was the small coin we now had. Since it was mixed in with many other ordinary items, no one realized any of it was esoteric or arcane—or even valuable at all.

The signet.

That small, coin-like item was among the objects in the lair sold to the merchant in Hammersfeld. Since its only purpose was to provide knowledge of the ancient dungeon's location, it wouldn't be detected as magic; the item would have been labeled as mundane, not magical.

However, that signet held the key to the immortal life of the undead.

The Lich King Vzerie would never return because he was destroyed during his final battle in Hallowdale Forest.

Nevertheless, the secrets Vzerie discovered in that dungeon, which the signet would reveal, would cut down the time it took me to become a powerful undead creature—a *nightwalker*—by several years. In fact, since I was already prepared, I would become one in just days once the phylactery was found and we returned to my keep in Minoras. The amulet contained the power, the dark energy, for the transformation.

If the lich had seen it, he must have used it and moved on; otherwise, it would have been found among the items the town had sold.

Strangely, Vzerie didn't have it. My only hope was that it remained in this dungeon.

Once we found the extra members to join our group, we would leave this city. We knew that others might still come after us following our attack at the last town, so we planned to stay in the Desolate Plains overnight.

There, tonight, I will stay up to analyze the signet.

Not only would it help open the door to the dungeon, it would also reveal its location …

* * *

ARGENT THE HUMAN

We were headed toward Hammersfeld City.

True to his word, Theodus had a squad of eight soldiers, plus a sergeant, join us at the town gate.

They saluted Grace, and she returned it.

"Hail, Argent. I am Thomas, Sergeant of the Guard, and this is the finest squad in all of Greenlove. We are proud to accompany you," Thomas said.

The other guards smiled at his compliment and nodded our way.

Thomas was not wrong.

They *were* among the finest guards of Greenlove Village. All of them were strong and fit. They each wore the splint mail of the guard, complete with full insignia to indicate their professional status and allegiance to the town. Carrying various melee and ranged weapons, they were a formidable group. I was glad they would be with us.

We would be noticeable as a small army, but it couldn't be helped. The mystery woman already had three confidants, and she clearly was looking for more.

We would need all the help we could get.

Our quarry was headed in the same direction the dwarf, Drek, had gone when we finished our last adventure. As I walked, I noticed the occasional wilting of plants and small dead animals near one side of the road—our mystery woman was heading this way as well. I don't know if this strange effect is from her or her mage accomplice, but it couldn't be just a coincidence.

"We see it too. Most peculiar, I have never seen its like," Clesus said.

The others nodded in affirmation.

"We must be careful. She is clearly building an army to help her. We need to do the same," I said.

"Drek?" Shivalt asked.

"Yes, if he is in Hammersfeld. Plus, finding more fighters and especially a thief would be good."

Shivalt laughed.

"Hammersfeld has some of the finest blacksmiths and taverns in all the realm. He will be here."

We all chuckled. He was right; Drek was probably still there.

It was early afternoon when we arrived at the city gate, and the guards waved us through. I stopped to speak with them.

"Pardon me, fine sir, but did a black-skinned woman and a mage pass this way?" I asked.

"Ah, fellow guards! From Greenlove, I see."

(The heraldry on Grace's armor and the other nine soldiers showed our allegiance.)

"Aye," said the Sergeant of the Guard—Thomas.

"Yes, we saw them. We don't remember most, but I remember her. I almost stopped her, something foul was about that woman and her companions—two of your guards were with them, I believe."

"Yes, *former* guards. They are all fugitives of Greenlove, and we are here to arrest them," Thomas said.

"Huh … What was the crime?"

"Murder and mayhem."

"Well then. We shall hold them and send word to Greenlove or you, should we come across them."

"Much obliged," Thomas nodded as he responded.

He glanced back at the rest of us and continued speaking to the Hammersfeld guard.

"We also believe they will not stay long and may be headed on. Is there a place here to recruit fellow sell-swords in the city? Perchance a thief as well?" Thomas asked.

The guard eyed him skeptically, but relented.

"Yes. I don't think much of those who sell their skills for coin, but that is not my place. Head to the Prancing Gnoll. Not only do they have good food and ale, but it's a gathering place for those with skills for let."

"Again, much obliged, sir."

Thomas waved, and the city guard returned the gesture, turning back to the entrance as we walked away.

After stopping for directions a few times, we finally found it in a busy section of the city.

As we walked in, we could see that it was lit by the lights from the windows, casting a musky look as dust filtered through the rays of sunlight. This was a commoner's bar, no rich or flamboyant attire present here. All were dressed in regular clothes, except for those who wished to reveal their professions.

We approached the bar.

The bar patrons at the Prancing Gnoll all took notice of our group. With my unusual look, a mage, an elf, and ten human guards, we resembled a squad of soldiers on the hunt—an accurate assumption. A couple of shady types quietly exited the tavern.

"What'll y'all be havin'?" the barman said.

He was tall and big. Not just fat, but also muscle. He had scars on his face, probably from stopping more than one bar fight in his day.

"How about a dozen full waterskins of water, and some information. All for a price, of course." I said.

"Well, I'll charge ya er ... two silver for each water-skin, so I reckon ..."

The answer was twenty-four, but I waited, since I didn't want to be rude.

"Ah, heck, jus' gimme two gold (which equals twenty silver pieces)."

"Deal."

"Now, the price of information ... What're ya lookin' for?"

He eyed the dozen of us. He knew we were not on a pleasure stroll.

"First, we are looking for sellswords to join us. A thief and some fighters, perhaps?"

"Hmm. Well, *that* I will give ya for free. Loras, over at that table," he said, pointing to a table where two men were playing cards. One had a dagger on his belt and a short spear on his back. He wore leather armor and had a scar running down the entire left side of his face. He was an average-looking man with short dark hair and a stylized mustache.

"He is a thief of some renown. Apparently of some decent morality as well ..."

"How so?" I asked.

"Well, I was gettin' ready for a ruckus when that black-skinned lady came in; she and her friends had the look of trouble, fer sure. She was looking for sell-swords, and I am guessing a thief as well. She approached Loras first and, well, I couldn't hear all the words, but a 'go to hell' was said by him in there some-where. He did not accept the black-skinned lady's offer. She was bad news. You could smell the evil on her."

He gave a look of distaste and spat on the ground behind his bar.

"Sounds like we have a winner," Clestus said.

I nodded yes.

"As for fighters, I would recommend the ones at that table," he pointed to the corner.

There were three men. One was a ranger, and the other two appeared to be fighters. You could tell he was a ranger because he was big and strong like a fighter, but his muscles seemed to have more endurance and less bulk. His armor and gear were all lightweight, including his studded leather armor. His leather boots were made for long strides.

"If that black-skinned lady is who you are here for, I have more information for ye …"

He raised his eyebrows and looked at me expectantly.

I reached into my bag and grabbed a gold piece. Changing my mind, I grabbed a platinum coin instead. This man was being quite helpful, and I wanted to encourage his forthrightness. I handed it to him.

He smiled and nodded approvingly, pocketing the coin.

"She and that mage fellow she was with had two of the Greenlove Village guards with them. They picked up a thief, a ranger, and two fighters. Must say, you are looking pretty similar in your way of doin' things …"

"Aye, that we be," said Roland, the guard that had come back from being turned to stone, "only not evil as hell."

The barkeep nodded and laughed.

"Yes. So I can see. Whelp, that is about all I got for ya —best o' luck on the recruitin'. I'm off to get yer wine-skins. Are y'all sure ya only want water?"

A few of the guards looked at each other.

Grace flipped the barkeep another gold.

"Maybe a few extra flasks of the good stuff, dear sir," she said.

He gave a mock salute and went off to get our

provisions. Several of our group nodded, smiling thanks to Grace.

I left the group to talk to Loras; no need to put him on edge with a squad of soldiers. Not that they were not already noticed, but talking to a lone woman was much less nerve-racking. He eyed me as I approached and put down his cards.

"Jim, I think I am done playing cards. I fold."

Jim smiled, took his meager winnings from the hand, and left. The pile of coins in front of Loras was much larger; he had clearly been winning. He motioned to the now-empty chair across from him, so I sat.

He said nothing, but was looking me over. Not in a sexual way, just noting details. This one was smart.

"I am sorry I stopped your game; you were clearly winning," I said.

He waved it off with a gesture of his hand, "Ah, not that hand though, no loss there … Anyway, how may I help your small army?" He glanced over at our group at the bar and back again.

"Well, have you heard the tale of the Lich, Vzerie, at Greenlove Village?"

"Aye. Was that your group?"

"It was. We lost a good man that day. A thief, by the name of Toad …"

He had a blank look on his face; clearly, the name didn't resonate with him.

"His actual name was Herbert, but he hated it—"

Loras started laughing; it was a contagious laugh, and I smiled broadly.

"Aye, me lass, that he did!" chuckling, he added, "Toad, huh? Heck, good a name as any. I am sorry to hear that; he was a good fellow and fairly good at cards too."

He sat back and took a swig of ale. I could see him eyeing me as he thought.

"So, you need a new thief. I tell you what, I knew Herbert, and if he agreed to work with you, then it does give you some goodwill—but I am not cheap to hire. I must be upfront about that. Of course, I need to know what I will be doing before I agree."

He sat back and waited. I knew this tactic, but didn't mind.

"We are hunting the black-skinned woman and her companions. They murdered two people in Greenlove and almost murdered a third. She is trouble, and I know you've already turned her down. We are going to bring them to justice, which will probably mean killing them."

He nodded, waiting for me to continue.

"Obviously, you will get an even share of any spoils from our trip. It will be split between our main party members only; the guards are on orders. Right now, that is a four-way split. However, we are looking for a friend of ours, a dwarf. Once we find him and hopefully hire you, it will become a six-way split. Plus …"

I reached into my *Bag of Holding*.

"Dagger or sling?" I asked.

He smiled.

"Sling, already have a magic dagger," he replied.

Loras stiffened for just a moment, then relaxed as I slowly pulled out my hand. I held the sling and a bag of stones for it, then handed it to him.

"A bonus for joining us. The stones are *fire-stones*. They have *Explosive Fireball* imbued into them. Toad used them quite effectively. I am sure he, as well as we, would be honored that they are going to you."

He nodded again.

"Hmm. Well, in that case, I accept. Besides, she was an evil little shite."

We both laughed.

"That is true," I said.

"Alright, let me get the rest of my stuff from my room, and I will meet you at the bar. How soon are we setting out?"

I raised my eyebrow.

"Ah, now, I got it. Back down in a tick."

He got up and went up the stairs to his room. Being a three-story building, I had assumed correctly that it was also a traveler's inn.

I went back to the group.

"OK, he is in. As soon as he gets back, we can head out."

I had a thought. I approached the barkeeper once more ...

"Excuse me, one last time, but have you seen a highly muscular dwarf in town? He stands about fifteen hands, fairly tall for a dwarf and incredibly muscular."

He thought a moment.

"There is someone by that description here. He isn't one you are looking to put away, is he?"

"No, no. He's a friend and former companion. We wish to recruit him to our cause."

The barkeep grunted and leaned below the counter. Now it was my turn to stiffen up and be ready ...

He came back up with a ledger. Flipping it open, he ran his finger down the parchment until he stopped on a name.

"Yessir, he is upstairs now. Had a bit of a bender, I'm afraid. I think he is sleeping it off. He is on the top floor, third door on the right. Drek is the name?"

"Yes, that's him. Thank you again."

He nodded, put the ledger back under the bar, and went down the bar to serve a drink.

While we were waiting for our provisions and Loras to return, I went up the stairs to fetch Drek.

The smell of beer and sweat gave way to a new scent as I ascended the stairs. Now it smelled of wood polish and musty air. I reached the top and went to the third door. I knocked and waited.

Then knocked again ...

Nothing.

I tried the handle, and it was locked. Looking around, I pulled out my lockpicks and got to work. Moments later, the latch slowly clicked open. Putting my hand on my sword, I gently pushed the door inward.

Drek lay, face down, on the bed. It sagged beneath his bulk as his body moved up and down as he snored like a bellows. Stepping forward, I looked at his hands.

No weapons in them; that is good. I shut the door behind me and approached him.

The smell of cheap booze permeated the room, and I wondered…

Just how much one had to drink to knock out a seventeen-stone dwarf?

No matter …

I cast *Instant Neutralize Poison* and waited.

"Hurmph!" Drek yelled as he bolted to his feet, eyes blurry at first, then focusing on me in newfound soberness.

"Argent!" He grabbed me in a bear hug.

Resisting the urge to pull away, I smiled and patted his back. His breath and clothes still reeked from his bender.

"Urgh, I d'ernt smell good. Sorry, me Lady Argent."

He took a step back from me.

"It's OK. We are in need of you once more, Drek. A necromancer and a drow have killed some townsfolk at Greenlove Village. We are hunting them."

He did not hesitate.

"Aye, me lass, I will clean up n' be down in jus' r' bit."

I nodded and left to head back downstairs.

After an eternal wait (I can't imagine that poor tub after he was done), Drek lumbered down the stairs.

He was wearing his full heavy plate mail and had his weapons with him. He held a giant, magical two-sided battleaxe, and on his belt were several magical throwing axes. A long black naginata was sheathed on his back—a magical "gift" from a *Wraith Lord* we had defeated early on during our adventure against the Lich, Vzerie. I could also see the magic rings on his fingers—a *Ring of Acid Resistance* and a *Ring of Strength*. With his already prodigious strength, combined with that ring, he was as powerful as a bull.

Several patrons eyed him and us, as we were not dressed for drinking, but for battle. We had all of our provisions by now, and Loras had returned long before Drek arrived. I was chaffing at the lost time, but they would smell us coming if Drek hadn't bathed.

We had tried to recruit the ranger and his two fighter friends, but they had been hired recently by someone else. Still, it was good that we at least added Loras and Drek to our team.

"Let the chase continue?" Clestus asked.

"Yes, let's go," I said.

We exited the pub and made our way down the streets to exit and follow our quarry. They had a healthy head start, but their lead was not insurmountable.

PART II

THE PURSUIT

CHAPTER 3

ARGENT THE HUMAN

uckily, whoever this drow woman and necromancer are, at least one of them left a wide trail of wilting vegetation to follow. I was really good at tracking, thanks to the incredible senses of a unicorn and over a hundred years of practice. Not that I needed it this time, as a five-meter-wide path made it apparent when they left the road and headed into the Plains of Desolation.

After an hour's walk, it became clear why it was called this.

It became more difficult to track them as the vegetation became increasingly sparse, soon reducing to nothing but sunbaked earth with a shrub or tree here and there. I could still see the trail that some of the party could not, but it became harder and harder, forcing us to slow down and, occasionally, even have to backtrack to find the trail again.

"I be wonderin'—is there perhaps a b'tter armor for the sun?" Drek groused.

Drek was sweating profusely, and our water consumption had gone up dramatically, even though Clestus had cast *Coolness* on everyone. The fatigue cost of keeping it on while marching was too high, so we had to do it in spurts to save our energy. It was still hot, and I knew the Bog of the Dead was a few leagues away still; we had the rest of the day's travel to get there. The good news is that the night would bring cool temperatures, and we should be able to reach the edge of the bog right around nightfall. That would be our camp for a short rest as we pursued our quarry.

Another boon was the pace of our foe. From the length of their strides and indentations, it was clear they were walking, not running. Clearly, they were not concerned about pursuit.

Whoever their leader was, they were smart, though. All of their party walked single-file, so we didn't know if they had more than the original four, but a good guess was that they did.

It was mostly flat, but we were reaching the crest of a small hill.

"Argent, do you see anything more of our quarry? Any guess how far they are ahead?" Shivalt asked.

Unlike the dwarf, he seemed more energetic now than when we started; his endurance was remarkable.

"No. If I had to guess, we should only be an hour or two behind. However, it would be best to catch them during the day."

I left unsaid what everyone knew—most drow had excellent night vision.

There was a sudden tremor, and the ground shook. An earthquake?

BOOM—AHHG!

The dwarf flew through the air as dirt and sand erupted from where he stood. He landed several meters away with a loud thump. Where he had stood was a monstrosity—

An *ankheg.*

Appearing like a giant caterpillar or bug, with a brownish chitinous shell and fearsome meter-long mandibles, it was a worthy foe.

I heard another scream and turned to see two more had come up from the ground. One had a town guard in its giant mandibles and quickly retreated into its tunnel.

The soldier's screams descended with it.

The other ankheg missed with its bite—sending Clestus sprawling into the dirt.

The one that now stood before me was massive. At thirty hands long and weighing at least sixty stone, its black insect-like eyes stared into mine. As it rushed forward on six legs, each ending in a wicked claw, I realized we would not be outrunning them. Its jaws spread, and it lunged for my head, closing them together with a loud SNAP.

I felt the rush of air from its attack near my head as I dodged left, drew my sword in one smooth motion, and struck its neck as it lunged at me.

Its head detached from its body.

The head hit the ground and rolled, still snapping its mandibles, while its body sprayed out a viscous black goo from its severed neck, its legs and body spasmodically twitching and thrashing in the dirt.

I turned to see Shivalt and Grace fighting one of them, while the rest of the guards were fighting the last one.

AHH!

A guard fell, covered in a black, sizzling acid that the creature spat up.

I rushed to his aid as the melee continued.

The sounds of combat were loud in the formerly quiet air.

As I knelt by the wounded guard, I started casting *Greater Healing* and *Neutralize Acid* on him. He had stopped screaming and was unconscious when I finished.

The other ankheg, fighting the guards, dropped from the many blows it received. It joined another guard that lay still beside it. The last ankheg was now running away at top speed like a six-legged ball of fire. Clestus had cast *Explosive Fireball* and *Flame Jet* on it. It slowed, then fell and lay still.

The guard I had just healed would live, but be scarred for life. However, the guard by the other ankheg was dead, torn almost in two.

"Ugh. The lil' bug tossed me but good," Drek said, walking over to me.

He had joined the melee at the end and now went to

retrieve his other gear, which had been scattered when he was vaulted through the air.

We looked at the hole the missing guard had been dragged into. It disappeared into blackness, then caved in dirt. The ankheg had collapsed the tunnel behind it.

There was no way to find him, and honestly, no chance he was still alive. Ankheg are like ants; they do not keep live prey. They kill and eat their prey or carry the corpse to their nest to feed their young.

I could feel the horror on everyone's minds, but we could do nothing more …

"Let's heal up and regroup. Once everyone is ready again, we should keep moving," Clestus finally said.

* * *

AFTER OUR BREAK TO cast some healing spells and eat a little food and water, we continued our journey through the Desolate Plains.

There was no wind and no clouds as we made our way through the hot plains. The ground was baked, with sparse, hearty sprigs of vegetation here and there. It was a wasteland, with only scorpions and bugs crawling on the ground and the occasional vulture flying overhead.

"Aggh! Could're be any more hot?" Drek asked.

"Aye, I could be wearing plate mail, I suppose," Shivalt said.

We all giggled as Drek gave him the stink eye.

The oppressive heat slowed our travel. Usually, I

would wait until nightfall, but our quarry was on the move and we had a lot of ground to cover. We were moving at a pretty good pace, so I hoped to catch up with them before nightfall, but time would tell…

"Water break," I said.

As the town guards formed a perimeter, they took turns drinking water while their counterparts kept a watchful eye on the horizon.

Clestus started casting *Coolness* spells on everyone again. It helped with the heat. As soon as he finished, we all resumed walking.

My exceptional sight and tracking skills allowed me to follow their trail. It was much harder to do now with the hard-baked ground and limited plant life. Still, with only a few double-backs, we were not far behind them.

As the sun started to dip, we made out the edge of the plains on the horizon, where sun-baked earth gave way to more vegetation.

Just beyond that would be the Bog of the Dead.

Not just a menacing name, it was called that for a reason. Many who ventured in never ventured back out. The tales of horrible monsters and dangerous quagmires were all too true. I was hoping they did not plan to go that way. There was now more vegetation, but not enough to conceal our presence. However, the trail was now easier to follow.

As the sun neared dusk, we slowed.

I could hear talking far in the distance.

The others saw my motion for quiet. As we crept closer, we all could hear them. Our enemy had made camp at the edge of the plain, just before the bog. Dusk would be upon us soon, the perfect time to attack. It was almost as if Clestus read my mind—

"We could attack at dusk. If we wait until night, it will be harder to follow them if they flee," he quietly said.

"Yes, let's set up a plan."

They had set up on a small knoll, offering a good view of the horizon. My keen vision and Clestus's *Hawk Vision* spell allowed us to see them from a safe distance. They had set a perimeter and had a half-dozen guards watching. Clearly, they found more sellswords. A tall, swarthy man in black leather armor stood near Kilrog and Onyx, chatting with them.

There was no way to approach without being seen, so we waited.

As the sun started its final dip toward the horizon, we were fortunate—it was behind us.

Clestus cast *Shape Light* and *Hush* spells on each of us, so that the sun would not reflect our light toward the enemy, and they would not hear our charge. Now we could move in, and they wouldn't notice us until we were almost on top of them. Our plan had to be as simple as it was foolhardy.

Grace and several of the others stayed near me to benefit from my resistance to evil and *Deflect Missile* aura. Once we got close, we broke into a run.

The plan almost worked.

As we neared, we slowed to a stop, and everyone fired arrows, sling stones, and bolts. They found their marks. With screams, two of their ranks went down. However, the missiles that were aimed at Onyx and the three men near her all came flying back at us!

She must have some aura like mine, only of *Reverse Missiles.*

The arrows and bolts narrowly missed Shivalt and me, but a guard that was just out of my protective aura caught an arrow to his chest and fell.

With no time to lose, we rushed them. Missile weapons were dropped as we closed to melee distance.

Onyx drew her jet-black great sword and cut a guard in two.

THWACK

As the two parts hit the ground, I could feel the fear. Her jet black sword pulsed with blood-red for a moment after the strike. No mere human could have done that; we are facing something clearly inhuman.

She started laughing as she drew closer to more guards. Even though her sword was over a meter long and probably weighed a full stone, she wielded it as though it were weightless. It spun and flashed through the air, moving at astonishing speeds towards the guards.

DREK

The town guard fell into two halves. Onyx had severed him just below the ribcage.

My God, what is she?

No time to ponder that, I readied my naginata. It was magical, which helped with aim and damage.

The crazy drow woman was smiling and laughing as she fought. I saw another guard step in as I thrust the naginata at her chest. With a lightning-fast sidestep, she swung her giant blade, blocking the other guard's sword. With an acrobatic spin, she swept the meter-long sword low and in an arc.

Screaming, the guard fell, chopped off at the knees.

It had gone through him as though he weren't even there. She continued the spin away from me as I brought down the curved blade tip of the naginata upon her. It hit the armor on her back as she moved out of its range. She almost dodged it, but I could see black blood splatter on the ground.

She smiled.

"Nicely done, dwarfy," she said.

If I were not in combat, I would laugh at the crude insult. Instead, I lunged in and swung the polearm hard against her. As it was just about to impact, she brought her sword up in front of her in a two-handed grip. My naginata felt like it hit a stone wall.

CRACK

The stump of my Naginata stayed in my hands, but the rest of it whirled into the approaching dusk.

What can destroy a magic weapon?

"What are ye?" I blurted out, readying my battleaxe.

She smiled and her eyes twinkled…

Then glowed a bright silver.

My body was wracked with pain as I could feel my organs and skin tightening and solidifying.

She was turning me to stone!

NO!

I fought against it as hard as I could … then it stopped.

Still unable to move, my vision slowly swam back into view; Onyx was now fighting Argent.

Their blades were singing as they parried and struck at each other. Soon, both were bleeding—Argent's red blood mixing with Onyx's black blood. Neither had a mortal wound, but both had found their mark.

I could only watch as Argent took on Onyx in swordplay.

ARGENT THE HUMAN

The battle was raging.

I can't tell if we are winning or losing, but Clestus and Kilrog were in an epic spell battle, and the town guards were clashing with their traitorous kin and the sellswords. I saw a guard fall, cut in two, by Onyx. She was the primary target and probably the most significant threat on the battlefield. So, I ran her way. A sellsword stepped between us.

"Die, you—"

I feigned an attack, then spun.

As he went to block my feint, I spun and hit him square in the body opposite his block. Were I a normal human woman, his armor may have stopped it.

However, I had the strength of a unicorn—more than double the strength of a strong man.

My blade sank over halfway through him, and I yanked it out as I continued onward.

Another of our guards fell, cut off at the knees as he fought with Onyx.

Drek stepped in at the same time, but her speed was incredible. As he brought down his naginata, she brought her greatsword between them. His naginata snapped in two against her greatsword, and he jumped back, pulling out his giant double-sided magic battleaxe.

Then he froze.

I could see him starting to turn greyish; she was turning him to stone!

Finally, I reached Onyx and, with a cry of anger, I swung my sword at her.

Onyx stopped her gaze attack and met my sword.

CLANG!

Our weapons shook as they hit each other. Anything not magical would have been rendered asunder at such an incredible impact. Only a vorpal weapon was sharp enough to break another magical weapon; both of ours survived.

We both registered shock.

She was clearly no human, and neither was I.

Onyx stepped back and looked at me in a new light. And it was not in a good way.

Her smile vanished, replaced by a look of pure evil and malice. She drew her sword back and swung at me.

As I blocked it, I was almost driven to my knees from the blow.

Her strength was greater than mine!

She continued hacking like a berserker, putting me on the defensive. Usually, a greatsword is not a fast weapon, but hers moved as though it were a mere shortsword made of pinewood.

It was mesmerizingly fast.

I managed to get in a few strikes, as did she. Stepping apart, we eyed each other as we circled. We were both injured, but our fight raged on.

From the corner of my eye, I saw one of our town guards fire a crossbow bolt at her. Just as it was about to hit Onyx, dead center, it spun and flew back to its origin.

The guard fell with a bolt in his chest.

What is she? I wondered.

I am your worst nightmare, *she replied in my head.*

My mouth hung open as she laughed.

BOOM

Fire erupted all over her as an *Explosive Fireball* from Clestus hit her. As the flames died away, she was still smiling; it had not affected her at all.

She rushed forward to strike me with that giant blade of hers.

Sidestepping, I parried it, sending a shiver through my bones.

How could she be so strong?

Her attacks were relentless, and she didn't tire. I managed to find an opening, however.

As she spun and manoeuvred for a killing blow on me, I saw a weakness—a way she moved that left her open.

I took it.

As I feigned and lunged, I spun low.

Oh no.

She had anticipated it; it was a ruse. As her "vulnerable" leg shifted away from my strike, her sword came down.

I barely had time to put my sword in the way, but I was off-balance; I knew her sword would not stop with my parry. My last vision was of her giant sword as it powered through my raised sword—and came down on my head …

ONYX—QUEEN OF THE NIGHTMARES

I had slain the strange silver-haired woman.

She had an appalling aura of good around her; it felt invigorating when my blade sank into her head. I had wanted to take her head as a trophy, but our enemy surged with a newfound anger after watching the woman in white armor go down. Her strength belied her size, which made me wonder what she really was; no human could be that strong. She clearly also had a vorpal weapon, or betwixt us would have been her broken sword.

We had to leave, though; my side was definitely losing. We had lost our other ex-town guard, all four sellswords, and the thief, but Telisgard and Kilrog still lived.

Between Kilrog's darkness spell and my innate darkness ability, the three of us escaped. The two of them climbed astride me as I changed into a *deathmare* and galloped away.

I wanted to stay and finish them, but they had gotten the upper hand on my sellswords. Even my thief had fallen to them—a shame.

I thought about the death and destruction as I slowed to a trot, then a walk. Smiling, my thoughts then turned to the signet.

As I was already immortal, being an undead demon from hell, the signet and the knowledge it would reveal were useless to me. However, having a powerful mage become a nightwalker was *extremely* valuable to me. He would surely be eager to aid me in my relentless pursuit to destroy all that was good and beautiful in this world. His new form would make him even more powerful.

One thing was now clear to me: what was left of my current company had shown its love for evil in all forms.

Now that Kilrog had deciphered the signet, we knew our destination. So, we were headed through the bog and toward a lonely ruin deep in its midst—

The "dungeon" that we sought now had a name: the Bastion of Garandel.

CHAPTER 4

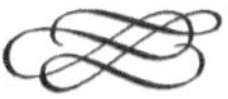

CLESTUS

We all saw Argent go down.

With a sickly crunch, Onyx's greatsword had powered through Argent's parry. The blade was slowed, but it cleaved through her leather helm and into her head.

She was slain.

In fury, I cast *Chain Lightning*, but if it injured the drow woman, I could not tell.

She disappeared into a giant area of darkness.

I heard a whinny and galloping hooves receding along with the now-moving patch of darkness. I continued to cast *Chain Lightning* into it until they were out of range. Several of Loras's *fire-stones* and missiles from the others joined my attack. With no target clear in the darkness, I feared most of our efforts were in vain.

I was right; the darkness quickly receded into the distance.

My *power-stones* depleted and my fatigue spent, I fell to my knees and panted. Using fatigue to power spells is like sprinting—uphill and through mud. As I tried to regain my breath, I saw the others trying to heal people, and Grace was holding Argent's head and crying.

It did not look good.

I unsteadily got to my feet and walked over.

The guard who was cut in two was dead, as was the one who was cut off at the knees. He had bled out before we could help him.

Another guard lay still with a bolt in his chest. He was making a horrible gurgling noise as he tried to breath. I rushed over and started casting *Greater Healing* as Shivalt removed the bolt from his chest.

Several of the enemy's sellswords, a former town guard, and their thief, lay dead as well.

Argent was not breathing. In desperation, I cast *Lend Vitality*. I could feel burning pain as I transferred some of my life force into Argent. The fact that it worked meant she was not completely dead—just "mostly" dead.

And, as everyone knows, mostly dead means some-what alive.

I lay down, my energy spent and my body now injured from my spell.

Passively, from the ground, I watched the others. They cared for the wounded and looted the dead.

I knew that Onyx and Kilrog were getting away. We

had decimated their party, but the heads of the snake were long gone. To make matters worse, Argent was our best tracker. Even though Shivalt was also an excellent tracker, the bog would hide their trail from him.

They were gone.

✳ ✳ ✳

ARGENT THE HUMAN

MY EYES SLOWLY OPENED, and I was confused because it was dark now, with just firelight twinkling in my vision. I could hear rain pattering onto something above me.

All of me hurt, and I had a splitting headache.

Suddenly, I remembered!

I tried to bolt upright, but I felt hands grabbing me and holding me still. Even though I had tried to lunge up, I could not, as I was tied in place. I tried to turn my head, but it would not move either.

"Don't move, Argent!" It was Grace's voice.

"You were mortally wounded, Argent. We don't know how you survived."

"Grace, wha … where? … Did she get away?"

I couldn't talk right; in fact, I wasn't even thinking straight. I remembered the fight starting and rushing to Drek's aid. The evil drow woman, the giant sword. Something about her evoked an intense fear in me …

Oww! My head!

I took a deep breath.

"How long?" I asked.

"Two days," Grace replied.

Two days.

The enemy had escaped. There was no hope of tracking them through a bog with a two-day head start.

I sighed.

"We have some good news, though," Clestus's voice said.

"Kilrog dropped his satchel in the melee. He survived my fire attacks, but his satchel didn't. It burned and fell from its straps. There was nothing of value, until I found this—"

A small signet came into my view as Clestus held it over me. I looked closely. Nothing seemed unusual about it; it was just a small seal set into a coin, with tiny writing in a language I didn't know. Maybe it was a heraldry of a distant land or something?

A distant land!

I tried to bolt up again and again realized my head had been immobilized.

Clestus chuckled.

"You got it, Argent! It is a crude map of where, hopefully, our quarry is headed. That signet was from the lich's treasure. I can't believe we missed something like that. It didn't look like anything—well, until now anyway."

Now that I was awake, I concentrated on healing myself. It was challenging, even with my innate healing abilities. Something was seriously wrong with my head.

I couldn't form spells; I could only will myself to heal. My head was making little popping sounds as it healed.

I wonder if I'm the only one who can hear that, or if it is audible to others?

I felt and heard the others as they started to untie me. As Grace removed the last straps from my head, I slowly got up. I felt a bit dizzy, but I was grateful just to be alive and well. I reached up and felt the bandages on my head.

The rest of the party looked at me.

They had set up a makeshift canopy of leaves and branches, along with shaped mud, to form an area of protection from the rain. They all looked well rested, but I noticed some of the guards still nursing wounds from the battle. At least Shivalt, Drek, Grace, and Clestus seemed unharmed.

Finally, as sunlight was just starting to form on the horizon, I felt mostly healed. The rain had tapered off to a light drizzle as I walked over to Drek, who was by the fire.

"Glad to see you are okay, Drek," I said.

"Hurmph, thanks be to you. A bit more'n I'd a been a pillar of stone," he said.

"Yeah, it must have killed you to watch the battle and not be able to move," Clestus said.

Drek merely nodded.

It turns out that he was partially petrified and unable to move until Clestus cast *Stone to Flesh* on him, bringing him back to normal.

"Aye, fer' sure. But, thanks ter' you I am not a statue. Thank ye both."

I went to nod, but pain flashed as I moved my head.

"Take it slow, Argent. You've been mostly dead for a couple of days now," Shivalt said.

"How bad was it?" I asked.

"Well, let's just say we know what unicorn brains look like now."

I gulped. Although not easily scared, a brush with death is never easy. I addressed the whole party next.

"I am glad we made it through. How many did we lose?"

"We lost three more town guards—Grifton, Wallard, and Smithson. Only Roland, Blaine, and Haragail remain on my squad. It appears none from your war party have been lost," said the Sergeant of the Guard, Thomas.

"I am so sorry, Thomas. We will avenge them, I promise."

To lose five out of eight men under your command must be devastating.

"In other news, the slingstones worked great," said a grimly smiling Loras.

He looked no worse for wear, but I noticed a large and incongruous feather sticking up out of his leather helm.

He saw my stare.

"Do you like my feather? Light as a feather..." he trailed off, smiling.

"It is a *Feather of Lightness,*" Clestus added.

I gasped.

I had heard of such a fantastic, magical artifact, but wasn't sure if it was real or just a legend. It was a powerful artifact that allowed its wearer to land like a feather without harm, and it also lightened the load of whatever was worn or carried to the weight of a feather —a unique and mighty artifact.

"Wow," was all I could say.

Loras beamed with pride.

"Besides that, and the signet in the burnt satchel Kilrog dropped, there were some healing potions, which we already used, a small ruby, and some coins. Not much else, though," Clestus said.

Things could have been worse.

Especially for me, I thought.

"Okay, let's get moving again if we're all ready."

"Aye, Argent. We were jus' a waitin' fer you to finish yer nap," Drek said, putting dirt on the dying fire.

I smiled.

"Alright, Clestus, lead the way ..."

* * *

THE MORNING SUN WAS WARM.

As we cleared the last of the Plains of Desolation, the ground became covered in grasses, then became damp, then turned to mud and swamp in only a league's journey. Everywhere around us were fetid swamp waters and the vegetation of the Bog of the Dead.

Our pace slowed as we looked for the firmest footing and sloshed through the waters.

Between magic and tracking skill, we were able to find paths that kept us from being submerged as we trekked through the slog of the bog.

I had taken the lead, with the fighters forming a perimeter around Clestus and Loras. Our progress was slowed down by the knee-to-waist-high waters, making our journey more challenging.

SPLOOSH! AHHH!

The area all around us erupted in a spray of water, and I heard several voices yell in alarm. Everywhere I looked, giant tentacles of plant-like "arms" had grabbed several members of the party.

At that moment, I saw Clestus transform into *Body of Flames*, and the tentacles surrounding him ignited and fell away. Thomas and Blaine were slashing madly at the tentacles that were immobilizing Roland and crushing him. Drek was writhing against the tentacles that held him fast, and Loras was cutting the ones that had him with his magical dagger.

All of this registered in a moment, as I felt the painful squeeze of tentacles that had instantly seized me from below.

FLASH

As I changed into a unicorn, my newfound size snapped the vines that were holding me. Without pause, I started shooting *Sunbolts* from my horn at the plants around me.

FZZT

A three-meter-wide, monstrous plant fell burning.

The creature resembled nothing more than a giant heap of rotting vegetation, with a large base tapering to a smaller "head". Sprouting from its body were multiple vine-like tentacles. It used them to strike and hold fast its prey, then crush them to death. I recognized these monsters immediately.

Shambling mounds.

Not highly intelligent, but they were almost invisible in a swamp. We were in trouble, for sure.

Loras had broken free and was busy cutting Haragail loose now, so neither saw the shambling mound that was heading their way.

FZZT

It caught on fire from the intense heat of my *Sunbolt* and flailed about before falling into the muck with a sizzling sound.

Drek had pulled free and was busy reducing the one that held him into multiple pieces with his giant axe. Already insanely strong, and now aided by his *Ring of Strength,* his giant double-sided axe was cutting them in two.

Clestus was helping the others by burning the tentacles off of them.

These monsters were impossible to see in the swamp and, being completely neutral in alignment, I was unable to detect them by any evil aura.

They were not evil—just hungry.

As the last of them was burned to a crisp, we took a look around. For once, we lost no one.

Haragail had a broken arm, but we managed to heal it enough for him to use it again.

FLASH

I transformed back into a human again and began casting healing spells on the injured.

"Well, that was fun," Grace said.

"Yeah, barrel of laughs," Thomas added.

After taking stock of ourselves, we marched on.

By mid-afternoon, we were near the location the signet indicated as our destination.

"Okay, let's go out in spokes from right here," Clestus said.

We were right on top of it. Whatever "it" was.

"Pair off, each team goes out in a different direction. Count to fifty paces, turn right, fifty more, and repeat until you are back here. If you see something, tell us when you get back."

We nodded at Clestus. He wasn't our designated leader, but he was smart, so we followed his plan.

The first time, we found nothing. So, we moved further in one direction and then another. Finally, we found it.

As we gathered in the center again, Thomas spoke.

"I saw a ruin in my area," he said, pointing in that direction.

"Probably about thirty paces or so …"

CHAPTER 5

ARGENT THE HUMAN

*C*lestus nodded.

"Alright, good job, everyone. Thomas, on you."

Thomas nodded and began walking toward the ruins he had seen. The rest of us made a formation and followed.

There were no more surprises, and soon the ruins came into view.

Long overgrown and with walls made of dried clay or mud, the building was not large, maybe twenty or so meters on each of its square sides. There was a set of stairs that headed up to an open archway.

As we ascended the stairs, Loras took the lead.

There was a trap that fired poison-tipped bolts when triggered, but it had already been triggered, and there was also a pit of spikes further in.

After a short walk, we reached the central area.

In a ten-by-ten-meter room, a pedestal stood as the clear focal point.

Loras raised a hand and started walking calmly to it. At first, I thought he was being overconfident until I remembered his *Feather of Lightness*. His footfalls were muffled and undetectable as he walked. Arriving at the pedestal, he examined it.

"Well, can you all see it?" he asked.

"See what, Loras?" Clestus replied.

"Exactly! Nothing. Whatever *it* was, they got it. I can see a round area without dust—maybe a hand across in width. So, they have what they came for," Loras finished.

He walked back across the room to us.

"Well, that was a bust. Ideas?" Clestus asked.

I shook my head. This was disappointing; we had all hoped for some indication of where they would go from here, but I was at a loss.

No one else seemed to have any ideas either.

"Let's head outside, see if they left any tracks or clues as they left," I added.

We headed back outside into the late afternoon, with Loras in the lead.

* * *

ONCE WE WERE ALL OUTSIDE, we saw the sky had turned an ominous grey. It would rain again soon.

WHINNY

Our weapons were up and ready in a flash.

I saw movement all around us.

Coming out from every side were giant all-black warhorses. They billowed smoke and had hooves, tails, and eyes of blazing fire. As they breathed, fire and smoke came from their mouths and nostrils. There were at least a dozen of them.

Nightmares.

Surrounding us, they stood watching us.

"Yoo hoo, my darlings."

We all turned.

There were Onyx and her companions—Kilrog the mage and the traitorous ex-town guard, Telisgard.

The look of shock on her face upon seeing me again could not be hidden.

"Well, well, well! It looks like I should have stayed to cut off that head after all, Kilrog."

He nodded.

"Easy enough to fix, though …"

She slowly pulled out her giant, intimidating blade.

The nightmares were snorting and chaffing at the ground with their hooves; it was clear they were ready for a fight.

"Why are you here? We never would have found you," Clestus asked her.

She laughed, long and hard.

"Oh my, it's like you don't know me at all! I am here because you offended me, of course. There is no world where I will let mere humans harm me and live to tell the tale!"

She had the most evil smile I had ever seen.

"So, I guess it is time—"

With a nod of her head, the nightmares charged.

FLASH

Once again, I was a unicorn.

Without a pause, I sent a *Sunbolt* flying from my horn. The first nightmare was charging at full gallop, leaving a trail of fire and black smoke in its wake.

My *Sunbolt* hit it right in the forehead.

FZZT—WHINNY

Its forehead sizzled and popped, brains and blood shot out as its head blew apart like an overripe melon hitting a wall. It stumbled over its forelegs and hit the sodden ground with a loud splash.

One down.

Another closed on Thomas, and, as he readied his sword, it breathed fire on him.

AHHH!

He screamed in agony as he was set ablaze. It didn't last long, though, as the nightmare hit him at full speed. His body flew several meters until it smacked against a tree. His smoldering body hung limply in its lower branches.

Drek saw this and took it out with several throwing axes. Meanwhile, Loras was using his sling to throw *fire-stones*. He stopped when he saw that the fire did not hurt them.

Clestus was casting *Chain Lightning* and brought down one of the nightmares, injuring a second one.

From across the clearing, Kilrog cast *Magic Missile,* and ten missiles zipped from his hands into Drek.

URGH!

Drek was knocked back several paces. The missiles burned his body, and I could see blood coming out of his armor.

Onyx took this moment to change as well.

I had been wondering what, exactly, she really was.

Now I wish I didn't know.

BOOM

In a burst of darkness and thunder, I felt fear sweep over me. As it passed, it smelled of a rotting corpse. Standing in her place was the biggest warhorse I had ever seen. Standing over twenty hands at the withers, it was a black that absorbed all light. Her eyes were the same all-silver that they were when she petrified people.

She made a retching sound, and a giant cone of blackness shot from her mouth. It resembled a twisting mass of black tendrils, almost looking alive. They engulfed Haragail, and he started screaming a low, plaintive wail. His body turned into a husk and blackened before my eyes.

As the blackness dissipated, his lifeless and shriveled corpse fell into the swamp.

Sweet Herates, a life-draining breath weapon!

I realized we couldn't win against that, so I shifted my focus to her next. I shot a *Sunbolt* from my horn, but she dodged aside, and it flew past her harmlessly, hitting the wet vegetation behind her.

She looked at me malevolently.

So, you are a unicorn! Oh my, I am going to enjoy finishing what we started earlier.

It communicated telepathically, just as I did.

I was scared.

I knew of nightmares; just as with unicorns, they were believed to be myths or fables. To see even one was terrifying enough, but to see a dozen, plus whatever fresh hell this being was—it was too much.

Without any concern for my safety, I charged Onyx.

She was bigger and stronger than I was, and I only hoped my horn could turn the tide of the battle.

FZZT—WHINNY

Direct hit!

Onyx's side burst in a blinding flash, and black blood shot out. She was wounded.

AHH!—I will kill you, you bitch!

The battle continued as we charged each other …

DREK

Several of the nightmares were down, but more were still up. Add in Onyx and her mage, and we had a hell of a fight on our hands. Plus, the traitor Telisgard was busy firing his bow at Argent.

Luckily for us, he didn't know about the unicorn's innate *Deflect Missiles* aura. So, he frustratedly kept "just missing" Argent as she charged his liege—Onyx.

A nightmare was headed my way as Kilrog fired *Magic Missiles* at me.

The spell is impossible to dodge, and his missiles hit me as though I had no armor at all. The pain was intense, and I stumbled. The nightmare sensed my vulnerability and was already starting to breath fire as it closed. So I did the only logical thing I could do: I charged as well.

As the fire-breath reached out to me, I shut my eyes and brought down my battle axe with all of my might. I felt it sink deep into something in front of me.

OOF!

I felt myself flying free from the ground for what felt like an eternity. I had enough time to think about how much I wished I had the *Feather of Lightness* right now.

WHAM—flop flop flop

I rolled to a stop and opened my eyes. Meters away was a nightmare with an axe driven through its head and down into its neck.

I stumbled over and retrieved it from the corpse. My face hurt from what seemed like the worst sunburn I had ever had, and I felt like I had been run over by a … well, a horse, I guess.

Looking about, I saw that Argent had wounded Onyx. It looked like she hit her with at least two *Sunbolts,* but they had missed each other in their first pass at jousting.

Onyx was now heading my way at full gallop.

I readied my axe and took a stance. Her speed was terrifying, and she stared at me with those eyes again.

Oh no, not again!

I couldn't move my feet and could feel the familiar tightening as I fought against her *Flesh to Stone* effect.

What in Crom's name is this demon?

My fate appeared sealed as Onyx covered the last meters to where I stood, rooted in place. She must weigh at least a hundred stone and was going faster than a racehorse.

This is it.

With the last of my will, I lifted my axe high overhead. As she blurred into a terrifying wall of blackness before me, I brought it down with all of my might.

She moved her head at the last moment, and it buried deep into her front flank instead—then she was on me.

BAM!—

* * *

ARGENT THE UNICORN

ONYX CONCEALED herself in an area of utter blackness.

Once again, I had to will my vision and the glowing sunlight of my body against an evil darkness. In it, I could just make her out.

FZZT

A full-powered bolt hit her in the side as she passed by. Unfortunately, I was not able to gore her with my horn. She had moved aside at the last moment. Still, I won this pass; she was injured again.

As I slowed and turned, I saw her crash into Drek—his battle axe sunk into her front, almost dead center.

With a sickening crack, I watched Drek fly like a rag doll, limbs akimbo, into the air. He landed with a splash in a boneless heap. There could be no doubt she had killed him.

I saw red.

Rage filled me at the thought of what this evil thing had done.

Shivalt skillfully dodged flames from the nightmares and used his bow and sword with practiced ease. Grace was holding her own as well, and I saw Loras throw a spear, taking out another wounded nightmare.

It looked like we were winning, or at least holding our own.

Onyx turned to me.

I guess this is the time we have been waiting for, eh ... Unicorn?

It is. You have done enough damage. Let's end this.

Her visage was less frightening now. Her left side was still smoking and bleeding from my two *Sunbolt* strikes, and Drek's axe was hanging from her front. It was lodged deep inside her, and blood was flowing freely from it.

She and I charged each other at the same time.

There is no kindness in battle, no regal rules of gamesmanship. I thought of this as I fired *Sunbolt* after *Sunbolt* as we closed.

I don't know if she was unable to dodge because she was charging straight at me, or if she was mortally wounded and resigned to a final death-charge, but most of my bolts hit true.

Her entire head was charred and sizzling as she breathed out that horrible black miasma. I could feel the cold stench of the *Deathtouch* in her breath weapon draining my life force … then we collided head-on.

BAM!—

I AWOKE to the sounds of battle all around me, and all of my body ached horribly. Slowly getting back on my four feet, I saw Kilrog going through a shimmering portal—he had cast *Dimension Door*—and then he vanished from sight. He had fled.

I heard a low chuckle in my mind.

Well, you just can't find good help nowadays …

I limped over to Onyx.

Her head was turned my way, but there was no fight left in her. I could feel her essence dying away, the evil lessening with each of her laboured breaths.

The wounds were grievous and mortal. Her whole left side, facing up toward the sky, was a sizzling and bloody, burnt mess. Drek's axe was almost completely buried in her now from our impact, and there was blackish blood pouring in spurts from where my horn had buried itself next to the axe, and then ripped free as we flew apart from the impact.

It was still difficult for me to breathe, and I was also severely injured; the impact had been massive, and Drek's double-sided axe—still lodged in Onyx's front—had cut me deeply as well.

Onyx had knocked me even harder than I had her. I felt her black blood dripping from my horn and into my left eye.

My horn had ripped her wide open.

As the last of her black blood burbled out of her, she spoke into my mind once more.

Kilrog is going to his Keep. It is at the base of the Eagle's Claw Mountain in Minoras, on the side of the setting sun.

Why are you telling me this?

Because he betrayed me... and ... because I am evil and know many more of you will die trying to kill him.

With a final rattling breath, she lay still.

Onyx was dead.

As I looked around, I could see the last of the nightmares turn and run away. The loss of their leader destroyed all their morale. That, or they only fought because she summoned them.

Either way, they were still pure evil.

We fired missile weapons and spells, and took out one more, but the rest galloped away and into the swamplands.

The air was filled with smoke from their passage.

All of Onyx's original party, save Kilrog, lay dead. I looked down with satisfaction at Telisgard's body in particular. Traitors to their own kind were the worst of the worst.

Of our original party, only Roland and Blaine of the town guard, along with Clestus, Grace, Loras, and Shivalt of the war party, remained with me.

I steeled myself and went to where Drek lay.

He was crumpled in a clearly lifeless heap. I nuzzled him, and he was dead. Not mostly dead, but dead-dead.

With tears, I realized the bravery of my companions.

How many had lost their lives fighting evil? How many more would die doing so in the days ahead? For the hundredth time, I wished that evil did not exist in our lands.

Tears welled up in my eyes—unicorn tears—that gently fell onto his lifeless body. Usually, these tears were my strongest healing power. They could mend paralysis, cure poison, and even revive someone on the brink of death, restoring them to health.

They fell uselessly upon Drek's corpse.

"Go to the great forge in the sky, Master Dwarf," Loras said.

"Aye, he be the bravest dwarf," Shivalt added, mimicking Drek's speech.

There was no treasure on our opponents, except for some coins. They had only mundane armor and equipment. Plus, whatever items Onyx had had died with her in her nightmare-warhorse form. Like me, those items would never be seen again upon death. She was now just a massive, dead horse lying in the muck.

Drek's armor would not fit anyone else, but we took

his magical axe, *Ring of Acid Resistance*, and *Ring of Strength.*

The axe and the Ring of Strength went to Roland, and the Ring of Acid Resistance was given to Loras.

I looked down again at Onyx and still wondered exactly what she was. A demon? A version of a nightmare?

I suppose we'll never know …

PART III

THE KEEP

CHAPTER 6

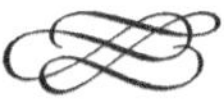

DARK WIZARD KILROG

I didn't want to abandon Onyx, but there had been no choice.

The unicorn had clearly mortally wounded her with its *Sunbolt* and goring attacks. As her nightmares turned and fled, it would be me against more than half a dozen of them—hardly a favorable outcome for me.

Besides, we had only stayed because of Onyx's desire for vengeance.

I had what I needed.

The small phylactery was the final piece; now I could complete my spell and transform into a night-walker: A terrifyingly large, undead creature that was devastating on its own. Add in my intelligence and spellcasting, and I would become an unstoppable foe!

These thoughts filled my mind as I walked from my *Dimension Door* toward my keep.

Along the parapets and bastions, guards were

stationed. Nothing human, of course, as those were kept in the cages as forced labor and life force for my necromantic spells. So far, we only had a few from the surrounding area, vagabonds and traders mostly—no one to be missed by a feudal lord or duke.

As I approached the main gate, the portcullis raised, and I walked in. I could see the murder holes above me and knew that boiling oil would be made ready for any invaders.

Reaching the central keep, I traveled through a long, hidden passage and entered a massive chamber. It was located far beneath the towering spire, at its foundation's base.

There, my pet was waiting for my return.

As I entered, the vibrations of my footfalls called to it. Moments later, the ground opened as its three-meter-wide maw burst from below.

The head of a *purple worm* appeared, dirt cascading off it as it rose. It was beautiful, with purplish skin twinkling in the *magelight* of the magical wall sconces.

After my spell was finished, the first of its kind, not only would I be undead, but so would my pet. Both of us would be able to drain the life force of the living—for all of eternity. As it turns out, I only needed hours, not days …

* * *

ARGENT THE HUMAN

AFTER THE BATTLE, I reverted to my human form. Sometimes I do it for tactical reasons, and other times I simply prefer being human.

I thought again of Onyx's last words to me. I never realized, until this moment, how evil can help good triumph.

By its nature, evil demands retribution on its enemies, perceived or real. The fact that Kilrog left Onyx to die was not lost on her. Sure, they had lost, but that isn't the point when you are evil.

The point, as always, is hatred of your foes—and those that betray you.

In this case, Onyx felt the betrayal and also hoped we would suffer and lose more people if she told us where he went; it turns out it wasn't far.

As *Dimension Door* is a spell that is harder and more costly in mana fatigue the further you go, it makes sense that he had not gone far. Besides, I am sure that was the direction they were headed before Onyx decided to set up an ambush for us.

Kilrog is going to his keep. It is at the base of the Eagle's Claw mountain in Minoras, on the side of the setting sun.

Her last words echoed in my head.

Now that we knew where to go, we took off through the bog again. We left Drek's body and those of our slain guards inside the ruins; better to lie there than to sink into the bog. With some final healing spells, we sat and ate our provisions and water. Grace took out the flask of brandywine and poured each of us a small cup.

I knew why.

"To those we have lost—we are forever thankful for their sacrifice against evil … Hail," Grace said.

"Hail!" we all echoed, downing our fingers of brandywine.

It burned going down, then settled in a warm sensation in my belly—just enough to be a physical reminder of the pain and death that Onyx and Kilrog had caused.

One down, and one to go …

"All right, we camp here and move out at first light," Clestus said.

We all knew that going through the bog at night was not a good idea. So, after a fitful night of sleep, we arose and started slogging through the marsh.

Eagle's Claw Mountain was visible on the horizon.

* * *

As we cleared the last of the bog, we saw Kilrog's Keep in the distance.

We were all exhausted from our trek, but we knew we couldn't wait. We had to get to the keep before nightfall to conduct our final surveillance. Then, as night fell, we would stage our attack.

We knew that whatever Kilrog had planned to do with the artifact he took, it was not in our best interest.

The keep was a marvel, probably built by dwarves long ago.

It was a solid structure. With ten-meter-high stone walls, parapets, and bastions along its length, and guards patrolling its top, it was a mini-castle. A tall spire with a bulbous top lay in the center of the keep. The main entrance had a pair of portcullises, with a kill zone between them.

We would not go that way.

The three sides were all like this, but the fourth side butted up to the sheer cliff face of the mountain above. It was quite the fortress.

We were in the forest, in a low depression, not far from it now. We could neither be seen nor heard at this distance.

Clestus cast *Hawk Eye* again, and he and I observed the keep's defenders.

I saw the defenders clearly now; they were mostly *hobgoblins*.

Hobgoblins are larger versions of their goblin kin, standing a full twenty hands tall, with hairy hides ranging from dark grey to a dark reddish-brown. Their skin, stretched over a muscular frame, was a dark red-orange. Wearing dark red leather armor, with a black crest of some kind, and carrying various weapons, they were intimidating foes. Unlike their goblin kin, they were well-organized and disciplined fighters—perfect guards for an evil wizard.

There were also some *bugbears* mixed in.

Even larger and more powerful, they were the strongest of the goblinoid races. Standing twenty-two hands high, they were broad-shouldered and even more muscular with yellow-brown hides and coarse, thick hair that was a dull red. With claws and noses that resembled those of bears, it was apparent how they earned their namesake.

"Hobgoblins and bugbears, that is going to make our assault harder," Clestus said.

"Yeah, but not impossible. We just have to get past them and into the main keep," I replied.

We stared for another minute, looking for weaknesses and ways in. It did not look good.

"Okay, let's brainstorm some ideas. One voice at a time, let's hear them," Clestus said.

"Well, we know that bugbears and hobgoblins have excellent night vision. So, dusk, once again, is our best time of attack," Shivalt said.

We all nodded in agreement.

"Agreed, time is confirmed, now … methodology?" Clestus asked.

"How about we teleport, one at a time, to where we can see there are no guards, somewhere past the walls?" Roland asked.

"Or, we could have Clestus cast *Walk Through Earth* on us and just walk through the walls?" Grace added.

"I could fall from the cliff above, using that *Feather of Lightness*, and then throw over a rope?" Loras asked.

We all sat quietly for a long moment.

"Well, I like the idea of just walking in through a wall, but what if he has a counter-spell on the wall? It could mean the entombment and death of the first person who goes." Clestus said.

"Teleporting?" I asked.

"A fine idea, doable for sure," Clestus said.

"How about teleporting me inside the keep first?" Loras added.

"That's actually a pretty clever idea," I said.

"You could put me on the other side of the wall, high up in the air, where it's clear, and I could fall behind it. You could use my location to send people through the wall, and I'd know it was safe," Loras added.

"How do we know that, if you are on the other side of the wall?" Roland asked.

"I've never tried to communicate that far telepathically, but how about if we test the distance now? Hopefully, the wall won't affect a willing receiver," I said.

Nods all around.

"Okay, let's try that, see if it works before making that the plan," Clestus said.

It was a plan, if my telepathy worked.

Loras walked a good fifty meters away and ducked behind a small boulder. I was still in human form, but my telepathy worked in either form.

Loras, can you hear me?

A moment later, I heard him in my mind. It was a lot harder than usual, but doable.

Yup, good to go!

He stood and walked back over to us, his smile telling the results of our telepathic test run to the others.

"Alright, let's find a position, just out of sight, but near where we want to go through the wall. I think that spot—" Clestus pointed at the wall where it joined the cliff face, then to a small area near the chasm on our side.

The spot he pointed to had an insurmountable crevice before it and the wall, so there was no guard above it. A small sliver of ground separated the wall from the chasm on their side.

"The plan is to teleport everyone to the wall at the edge of the crevice. From there, I will send up Loras. When he and Argent are communicating and, hopefully, the coast is clear, we can start sending people through the wall."

We all nodded.

Without any more conversation, we quietly headed to the spot he pointed at. There was still plenty of vegetation to help hide our advance.

It was a bit of a hike, as we moved slowly to avoid being spotted or making excessive noise. The guards were actually rather inattentive, likely due to the monotony of seeing nothing for days and weeks on end.

We arrived without issues.

Clestus and I looked out at the wall. It still looked like our best plan.

"Ready, Argent?"

I gave Clestus the thumbs-up.

He pointed at me, and I felt the familiar sensation of his *Teleport Other* spell. I did not resist.

As I apparated on the ground, I felt dizzy. Before me, a mere four or five hands away, was a blackness falling deep into the earth. I stepped back one step to feel the cold stone of the wall. I am not afraid of heights, but I am not an idiot either.

After several more popping sounds, we were all on the outside of the stone wall, with the crevice only a meter or so away.

Clestus pointed at Loras, who merely nodded his assent.

"Loras, make a wish," Clestus said quietly, motioning his way.

POP

Loras was gone.

We waited …

Hi, Argent. This side is clear and quiet. We got lucky.

"He's ready, we're clear," I said.

Clestus started casting *Walk Through Earth* on each of us. It was weird to see someone walk into a wall and disappear.

I went second to last.

With a nod to Clestus, I felt a strange sensation. Walking forward and holding my breath, I entered the wall and into utter darkness. I could feel the stone moving around me as I walked.

Suddenly, there was light; I had made it through. Right behind me, Clestus appeared.

"That was easy," Loras said.

"You just had to say that, didn't you?" Grace added.

He smiled, and we started toward the central area of the keep. I am not superstitious, but this part had gone pretty well so far—too well.

We got to the edge of another interior wall, and Loras peered around the edge, quickly pulling back.

"Okay, we have two hobgoblins guarding the entrance to the central keep—" he looked at us for guidance.

"That works. We will need to rush in after hitting them. If they go down without raising the alarm, we continue in. If the alarm is raised, we go in anyway … So, I guess we have a plan, for better or worse," Clestus said.

Loras prepared his spear, while Grace, Shivalt, and I readied our bows. Roland and Blaine had crossbows.

Clestus got ready to cast *Wall of Silence*. This is a spell that encircles an area. Once activated, those inside cannot hear sounds from outside, and people outside cannot hear those inside.

There were no other guards nearby, as they did not expect an attack from within the walls. Clestus finished casting, nodded, and raised his arm. We all nodded back; everyone was ready to step out and fire.

His arm went down—

TWANG

Our arrows, bolts, and Loras's spear all hit them. Resembling a couple of big pincushions, the two hobgoblins silently went down. Without delay, we rushed through the door to go inside the keep—dragging the hobgoblins' bodies in with us.

Once inside, we shut the sturdy door. Ahead, we could see a hallway ending with another stout wooden door.

"Looks like these two have nothing of value, only a few coins," Loras said as he put the coins in a bag and pulled his spear free.

"Let's get moving then. Loras, take the lead," Clestus ordered.

Grace, Shivalt, Roland, Blaine, and I made a phalanx around Clestus as we moved. We had melee weapons out now.

The door was locked, but Loras made quick work of it. As it opened, it creaked.

The room was cavernous, with high ceilings and a wide circular shape.

Loras made an audible gasp.

A giant pile of treasure lay before us in the center of the room. We scanned the walls, floor, and ceiling. Surely this was some sort of trap. Loras moved forward, tapping ahead of himself with his short spear. He had fashioned a bag at the end, one filled with rocks. He had done this before …

Tap tap tap

SNAP

The ground in front of him fell open to a pit of stakes below.

Then, the treasure pile began to shift before our eyes … and stood.

A resplendent creature stood before us. It was at least fifty hands tall and must weigh over four hundred stone. Its body was earth, rock, and precious metals— what we thought was treasure. Its two multi-faceted gemlike eyes glowered at us, and its mouth and face were cold and expressionless. This creature was made of whatever materials were used in its creation when it was brought to the material plane. Surely, Kilrog had used gems and coins as a lure for interlopers. Vaguely humanoid in shape, it stood fully upright now.

An *earth elemental.*

It wasted no time in attacking us.

As it came around the pit, it rushed forward, and it built up speed.

Loras sprinted to the side and readied his sling. Shivalt, Grace, and I stood our ground. Clestus, predictably, turned into a *Body of Flames.*

It roared, a horrible grinding stone sound that resembled the cascade of an earthquake. As it got near us, Grace broke right and hit it with her sword. A blast of fire came from its side as Loras's *fire-stone* hit it. My sword also careened off its solid body, seemingly doing little harm. Roland's axe bit into its side as it smacked him with one arm, knocking him down. Luckily, he partially dodged it, so he was still in the game.

FLASH

Changing into a unicorn was my best bet. Knowing my sword was of limited use, I figured my arrows would not fare much better. Clestus cast *Stone to Flesh* on it, and I saw a spot on it turn into a fleshy section, so I fired a *Sunbolt* into that as it turned on Loras.

FZZT—CRACK

A chunk of its side came off, with a spray of dirt, coins, gems, and big chunks of weird-looking "flesh".

It roared again.

The others could see their strikes and fire did negligible damage to it, so they were all taking turns taunting it to go after them.

It picked Loras this time and was catching up to him. Right as it was almost to him, he vaulted over the pit using his spear like a pole jumper. The elemental reached out and hit him as he was in mid-air. He cried out and was flung the rest of the way across the pit.

There was a loud crash as the elemental stumbled into the pit. Falling to the ground below, we heard the spikes snap. When it stood, it was still visible from the shoulders up; it was huge. As it started to climb out, Clestus kept casting Stone to Flesh, and I kept hitting the fleshy spots that it was making on the creature.

As it climbed out from the pit, Clestus targeted its leg.

FZZT

With a pulverizing spray of stone, precious metals, and dirt, it lost its balance and cartwheeled back into the pit. I galloped quickly to the side of the pit, and Clestus and I continued our attacks.

ROAR

My ears hurt from the sound of its roar in the chamber, but our attacks were working. The beast now had no legs below the knees.

THWAP

I saw an arrow zip past my face from the side. It had shifted slightly and missed by mere inches.

My *Deflect Missiles* aura had saved me again.

Turning, I saw a group of hobgoblins entering the room.

Shivalt stepped up and cut one across the chest, and it fell. The one next to him swung at Shivalt as he parried.

The other four ran past and were engaging Grace, Roland, Blaine, and Loras (who had just stood).

FZZT

Another hobgoblin fell in a blinding flash, his body sizzling as it struck the earth.

CRUNCH

The elemental was starting to pull itself from the pit, so I turned my attention to it. Clestus saw it too, so we went back to fighting it.

The others were on their own to fight the hobgoblins.

As it pulled on the edge of the pit, Clestus cast again. Seeing its now earthen/fleshy hand, I aimed my horn—

FZZT

It slipped back down and was starting to pull out again with its other hand and the stump of its other arm.

Another casting and …

FZZT

It fell into the pit. Now, with no hands or legs to use, it slowly started pulling itself up by its arms.

After many *Stone to Flesh* spells, combined with my *Sunbolts*, it fell into the pit. Now with no arms or legs, it was no longer a threat.

Clestus and I turned as one to the hobgoblins

pouring into the room. Clearly, at least a local alarm had been raised, and more would be coming. We had to move, or we would be overwhelmed. We fell back to the next door, viciously fighting the hobgoblins.

Loras got to work on the lock, while the rest of the party made a semi-circle around him and the door.

I continued to run around the room, taking out one at a time with well-placed *Sunbolts*. Being much faster than they were, it was a good tactic. However, their numbers were increasing faster than we could kill them. Plus, bugbears were starting to come into the giant room.

Time was running out.

"Go, go, go!" Clestus yelled.

The door was open now, and the party was going through. With a final effort, I charged the open door. There were several hobgoblins in my way, but luckily, they were concentrating on the rest of the party and not facing me. I felt them hit my front and then under-hoof as I ran through them into the three-meter-wide hallway beyond.

Clestus was casting *Shape Earth*, but the spell took a few seconds, even at his skill level. The hobgoblins were stuck at the doorway—a practical choke point, as we had hoped.

Shivalt and Grace were holding the hobgoblins at bay, but I could see they were bleeding. Both had taken some damage in the melee.

There was a deafening crash as the roof above the doorway started to fall. Shivalt and Grace moved back quickly as the air filled with dust and debris; we were all blind now.

As the dust cleared, we heard a deafening silence, followed by the tinkling of rocks and pebbles still falling from the roof. The area behind us was now a wall of rubble.

FLASH

As a hallway is not ideal for a unicorn, it was time to switch back to being human again.

"Hold still; let's heal up," I said.

I cast *Greater Healing* on Shivalt while Clestus worked on healing Roland, Blaine, and Grace. Loras must have some sort of magical luck. Except for a bruised rib cage from the elemental, he was fine.

Now healed up, we drank water and reformed our party. A long hallway lay ahead of us.

Having a flashback to a long hallway in the lich's dungeon, I remembered that trap vividly.

"Careful, Loras," I said.

He smiled, more a forced grimace really, as he took the lead. His famous bag-on-a-spear once again led the way.

We made it to the next door safely. Loras picked the lock, and we opened the wooden door. There was another large chamber, this time with a vast opening in the ceiling above. Another massive pile of treasure awaited us. This time, the room was also littered with the long-dead bodies of adventurers, and the weapons and armor of the long-deceased were on the skeletons.

"Really, again?" Loras said.

The walls all had a strange lumpy texture. Black protuberances and shiny, scale-like surfaces reflected at us in the dying rays of the sun. On the other side of the chamber, another three-meter-wide hallway beckoned.

"What now, boss?" Roland said to Clestus.

"Let's skirt the treasure pile and head to the hallway, it must be a trap of some kind ..." Clestus looked at Loras as he trailed off. Loras nodded his head in agreement.

We started walking around the edge of the chamber to get to the far hallway. The air was still, but there was a cloying smell— a smell of death and decay. As I walked, I eyed the wide-open roof, the treasure pile, the walls, and even the floor. I could feel evil nearby.

"Something is here," I said.

The others nodded at my warning.

Something shifted, just slightly, on the wall across from us.

Shivalt reacted with astonishing speed. One moment his sword was drawn, and in the next it was sheathed and his bow unlimbered, already notching an arrow.

THWAP

The wall exploded outward from where his arrow struck.

CRAWKK!

Wings unfurled as a small section of the wall revealed its true nature— a *black dragon*.

This one was an adolescent, thankfully. Still, it was huge. Almost sixty hands long, it was a scaly, black-skinned creature with dead-black eyes and a huge wingspan. Its mouth had large fangs, and all four legs ended in deadly claws.

With a retching sound, it spewed a concentrated stream of blackish gunk all over Loras. The force of its breath weapon knocked him down, covering him in black muck.

Shivalt rushed forward as it took to the air, barely missing its underside with his sword. Clestus fired *Explosive fireballs* from his *Staff of Immolation* while the rest of us pulled missile weapons. Suddenly, an area of utter blackness sprang all around it, one of the advantages a black dragon could do once a day.

With it in the air, I knew what I needed to do—

FLASH

As a unicorn again, I fired a *Sunbolt* into where I thought it was—

FZZT

CRAWKK!

Its outline was briefly visible in the light of the *Sunbolt*, and I heard everyone open fire at once. Clestus's *Explosive Fireball* and Loras's *fire-stones* both hit it in a flash of light and fire. Someone must have hit a wing, because it dropped roughly to the ground with a thud. As Shivalt charged it with his sword out (how is he so fast?), it spewed acid breath again. Shivalt dodged to the side, and only some of the spray hit him. Crying out in pain, he plunged his sword deep into its side as it snapped its head around at him.

Just like Shivalt's attack, the dragon didn't miss either.

The serrated jaws and sharp teeth of the dragon clamped onto Shivalt's torso and shook him viciously until something tore loose, causing him to fly to the side.

Shivalt lay in a crumpled heap, unmoving.

Meanwhile, Loras hit its hindquarters with another *fire-stone*, and I saw one of Grace's arrows stuck in its thick scales.

FZZT

Another part of it sizzled from my attacks.

Roland and Blaine charged forward and began attacking it. Although dragons are magical and thus require something made of magic to hurt them, all but Blaine's sword were enchanted.

The dragon spun in a quick circle, and its tail knocked Roland and Blaine back several meters. The beast was powerful.

Suddenly, as it opened its maw to bite Blaine, its head exploded in a shower of black gore.

Clestus had put an *Explosive Fireball* into its open mouth. A fortunate shot, but luck we were thankful for. We watched its headless body thrash about and then lie still ...

"That is so gross," Loras said.

Clestus was spraying him with a *Create Water* spell, and the blackish muck was coming off him.

"Thank you all for giving me that ring. I am quite

sure I would be a sizzling puddle if I weren't wearing it!"

I went over to Shivalt.

His crumpled and bloody body lay still, and I could sense he was dying.

Kneeling on my front legs, I cried tears of healing onto him. I lifted my head and saw in my peripheral vision that Roland was awake and being given healing spells and potions. Luckily, we lost no one in this fight.

Strangely, the dragon had stayed to fight.

Why would it do that?

Dragons were wise, and this one definitely knew it was outnumbered. All it had to do was stay still, and we never would have spotted it.

As I looked closer at the treasure pile, I realized something. This was a youth; its adult parent was probably out looking for food. It could return at any moment.

Studying the indentation of a gigantic body on the pile, I saw something that looked out of place. Blackish lumps lay partially buried in the enormous indentation on the top of the pile.

Dragon eggs.

The adolescent was guarding the eggs, and the mother would be back soon. We didn't want to be here when she arrived.

When I looked over at Clestus, I could tell he had come to the same conclusion.

"We need to go, right now!" Clestus said to everyone.

Grace and Roland put Shivalt's unconscious body on me, and we rushed into the corridor. There would be time for looting treasure later; we had to stop Kilrog before he did whatever spell he had been working on for so long. We reached a turn in the hallway and followed it to the right. Up ahead was yet another door.

It turns out it was a good thing that we left when we did—

CRAWKK!

The walls shook with the fury of the black dragon's scream. I don't know how big she is, but if the thirty-meter-wide imprint on the treasure pile was any clue, she was at least an *ancient dragon.*

There would have been no surviving a battle with her.

Loras managed to pick the lock once more, and we found ourselves at the base of the impressive, prominent spire we had seen from afar. There was a turret of stairs visible in the center of the room.

We watched and waited. It looked too easy.

As we waited, Shivalt began to stir. Grace stroked his hair as his eyes opened once more ...

CHAPTER 7

THE NIGHTCRAWLER

y master had changed me.

No longer a living thing, I waited, silently, to kill any life that crossed my path—lying deep underground, sensing the vibrations above me.

I could sense the evil darkness within me, waiting and longing to be unleashed …

* * *

ARGENT THE UNICORN

THE ROOM YAWNED OPEN WIDE before us.

This chamber was even bigger than the spire above it. We could see the enormous columns of stone that jutted up to support it—every few meters, another three-meter-wide column. The room itself was even bigger than the twenty-meter radius of the spire. It was at least a hundred meters across.

Why such a big, empty room?

The floor was entirely dirt, except for a twenty-meter inner diameter, which was made of stone flooring.

Nothing looked out of place, although the rough, uneven dirt floor reminded me of an unfinished cellar, albeit an enormous one.

WHINNY

I shook my head vigorously. The rest of the party nodded in understanding. They knew me well enough to understand my warning, even without telepathy. Something evil was here.

"OK, let's do this. Loras …" Clestus said.

Loras nodded and took the lead.

Tap, tap, tap

We moved across the dirt.

Tap, tap, tap

We were almost to the stone floor.

Tap, tap, tink

We had reached the stone flooring. I am not sure why that matters, but it felt reassuring for some reason that I couldn't explain. As Roland was the last of us to step off the dirt, I felt relieved that nothing untoward had occurred.

The air suddenly went cold, and I felt the horrible despair that only the life drain of the undead could cause.

BOOM!

Everything behind me erupted in a massive explosion of debris. I closed my eyes as jagged shards of stone pelted me. Amid the pain, I felt numerous deep cuts. I spun around to see the most horrifying thing I had ever witnessed.

Loras had been swallowed whole by a giant, inky-black worm. I could hear his screams as he went into its gullet.

Resembling a purple worm, its three-meter maw had swallowed him whole as it came up through the stone floor. It finished coming out, all forty meters of it. It had dirt and debris all over it, and its tail ended in a viscous-looking stinger, much like a scorpion's tail only much larger.

FZZT

My *Sunbolt* struck its side and sizzled. Everyone drew melee weapons and charged it.

Clestus turned into a body of flames and started using *Flame Jet* on it.

The good news was that our magic spells and enchanted weapons were hurting it. The bad news was that it was HUGE. As some kind of undead version of a purple worm, standard non-magical weapons would not harm it. Luckily, almost all of ours were magical.

As it curled like an earthworm, its stinger flashed out and impaled Blaine.

He coughed up blood and fell prostrate as the stinger came out.

Rushing to his aid, I cried unicorn tears on him.

They would stop the poison and aid his healing if he survived.

With no more time to spare, I turned on our nemesis.

Roland took a big chunk out of it with Drek's giant axe, and I saw Clestus's fiery body running along its flank, a *Flame Jet* burning its side as he went. Grace and Shivalt were hacking at it as well. It curled and flung out its tail, knocking Grace back several meters.

FZZT

I kept at a distance and fired *Sunbolt* after *Sunbolt* into it.

The creature convulsed as there was a splash of black blood coming out from inside it. A grotesque humanoid form, covered in black blood, pushed out from the slit in its side.

It was Loras!

He had cut his way out!

Loras ran a few meters away and then turned his sling on it. Fiery explosions from his sling added to the bedlam. The creature was clearly wounded and slowing down. With a sudden flip, it dived into the ground face first and began tunneling. Just as the last of it was heading into the ground, Shivalt swiped his sword.

The tail with the stinger flew off.

Silence filled the air. All we could hear was our heavy breathing.

I rushed to Blaine.

He was breathing. Good, he was going to make it.

Shivalt and Grace roughly tossed him over my back,

and we quickly entered the stairwell. I saw that Loras had already cleared the first few steps with Roland.

We went up a few steps, just in case the worm came back. There we rested, waiting for Blaine to regain consciousness.

I was healing myself now and watching the others. Roland and Loras were guarding above us while Shivalt and Grace guarded below. Clestus was beside me, ready to engage in either direction, and once again using *Create Water* to spray muck off Loras.

* * *

"Uʜʜ …" Blaine spoke as his eyes finally opened.

"Welcome back, Blaine," Grace said.

"Thanks, I thought that was it," he replied.

"Glad you are okay. Sorry to rush things, but are you able to keep going?"

"Aye, I am," he said, while standing up.

We all prepared for our ascent of the stairs.

The stairs went up clockwise. They were designed this way so that a right-handed attacker above would have the advantage over those below.

I saw that the steps were narrow and steep.

FLASH

Knowing my limitations, I reverted to being a person again.

We climbed the worn, stone steps ever higher. Loras was in the lead, slowly analyzing his every step, the walls, the floor, the ceiling. Halfway up, he stopped. He bent down to look closely at the stone steps. He motioned to one and carefully stepped over it to the next higher step. We all followed in his footsteps, literally.

He found several more steps that he was wary of, but we rounded a corner and saw the top.

Finally, we were at the top of what must be the lone spire we saw earlier. There was no door this time; it just opened into a large, circular chamber, about fifty meters across and a good ten meters high. Above our heads as we exited the stairs was a large boulder, held in place by a lever going into the wall. If it had been released, probably by the steps we crossed over without touching, it would have fallen and started down the staircase.

It could have killed most or all of us.

We paused to observe our surroundings. Around the circular room, large openings lined the perimeter. These openings extended from floor to ceiling and lacked guardrails. Anyone stepping through the one-meter-wide gaps would fall to certain death. About five meters of wall separated each opening.

It was a strange chamber. The faint, diffuse light from the outside moon illuminated it, casting shifting shadows as it moved.

My excellent night vision was almost as good as my daytime vision, but I knew the other party members could not see as well.

Now, my senses were screaming at me; something *very* evil was here.

"Evil is here, be ready," I said.

Everyone moved closer to me; they all knew of my *Protection From Evil* aura. Once they were close to me, I changed—

FLASH

I turned into a unicorn and willed myself to continue letting off an aura of sunlight.

As the room suddenly filled with light, the walls seemed to disintegrate. Forms detached from the walls: we could see their melted-looking bodies as they stepped onto the cold, stone floor.

Bodaks.

These horrible creatures were once people. Being slain by absolute evil, they now were a caricature of their former selves, with sexless, greyish bodies, devoid of any hair and having a melted appearance; their empty, white eyes stared at us in a perpetual state of madness and horror. They moved slowly at first, with those eyes staring into ours.

I felt a coldness that could only be one thing—a *Death Gaze.*

Worse than what Onyx could do, if I failed to resist its effects, I would die instantly. My body would turn into a bodak within just a day.

Those near me felt an extra layer of *Protection from Evil*, including against the bodaks' *Death Gaze.* Thankfully, everyone had stepped near me.

The bodaks' faces took on an expression of even greater torment, and we could see their skin smoking.

My innate *Sunlight* effect was just like the real thing, making their skin start burning.

They broke into a sprint, straight for us.

FZZT

One burst into flames from my *Sunbolt*, as a second did the same from Clestus's *Explosive Fireball*. His fireball knocked another one over and lit it aflame as well.

Shivalt swung at one as it dodged him, cutting off its arm in the process. I saw Roland cleave one in two. Between his already strong frame, the *Ring of Strength*, and Drek's battleaxe, he was a formidable ally. Grace and Blaine were holding their own, but I could tell Blaine had lost some lifeforce to one of them; he was slowing.

Their numbers were dwindling as we hit them with melee weapons and spells. Suddenly, I couldn't see as the entire area was enshrouded in blackness. Someone had cast *Darkness*.

I stopped my attacks and resisted it with all of my will. After several seconds, the room returned to daylight.

Blaine was on the ground, shriveled to a husk. A bodak crouched over him.

As it stood, Roland took its head off with a swoosh of the giant battleaxe.

A new feeling of coldness and death permeated the room as my *Sunlight* dimmed again, casting the room back into a twilight of shadows. Something *powerful* was near, and a shadow fell over us all.

Looking up, I saw something that I never thought was real.

A *nightwalker.*

Standing over sixty hands tall, it was a humanoid shape with glowing, electric blue eyes and unnaturally long arms ending in vicious, sharp talons. Its body was like Onyx's, utter black that seemed to absorb all light. It was an undead colossus with unimaginable power.

It raised its hands, and they shimmered with blackness. A low moaning sound came from the floor.

Two wraiths, smoky and darkly ethereal beings with glowing red eyes, slowly rose from the ground. These undead creatures can draw the life force from the living, making them quite ominous and formidable.

I aimed my horn and fired at one, but it dodged at the last moment. My *Sunbolt* sizzled into the wall behind it.

Magic missiles flew from the already outstretched hand of the nightwalker. I felt ten explosions in my flank as I fired a *Sunbolt* into it.

FZZT—BBBOOM

Searing pain filled me as ten small exploding daggers blew blood and chunks of flesh from my side.

I could not take another hit like that.

Clestus's *Fireballs* and *Chain Lightning* were having little effect on it. I could see that my *Sunbolts* were causing it extreme harm, though.

I rushed forward to gore it with my horn, and it opened its arms wide and waited.

What was it planning?

At full gallop, I dropped my horn and jumped for its midsection. Just as it was about to sink in, the night-walker reappeared two meters away and raked its claw against my wounded right flank as I passed. It must have cast *Blink*, a defensive spell.

I landed and managed to keep on my feet. The pain was unbearable, and my side was leaking blood; its claw had caused grievous damage to me.

I finally understood who or what this was.

He reached out telepathically to me—

Ha, ha, ha. You figured it out. No worries, no one will leave here alive to tell anyone.

Kilrog. So this is what you have become? An undead monster?

Yes. Now, would you kindly die, you loathsome creature!

Kilrog cast *Insect Plague* and sprayed insects into my wounded side, and I could feel thousands of insects burrowing into my flesh. The pain was more than I could bear; I staggered into the wall. Blazing with sunlight, I scraped hard into it, dislodging some of the bugs that hadn't burrowed in yet.

Crying in agony, I fell.

I cast *Cure Disease*, as I knew that was the counter to what he had cast on me. I felt the insects dying in mass, popping out of my flesh with a horrible-smelling greenish goo. From my side on the cold stone floor, I watched the battle rage; I was too weak to help as I concentrated on the spell that may keep me alive.

Kilrog's mirth was cut short as Roland took off his left arm at the elbow with his battleaxe.

Ahhh!

Kilrog's agony would have been enjoyable, but I was in more agony than he.

Clestus had cast *Protection From Evil,* and the party was winning the fight. The bodaks were no more, and only one wraith still stood.

Grace and Shivalt turned on Kilrog and moved in. I saw Shivalt freeze in place; a *Total Paralysis* spell had struck him. Then I saw Grace slice into Kilrog's leg with her sword. It swiveled its massively long arm and hit her shield with its remaining claw. Its force knocked her down.

Loras's spear flew across the room and buried deep into Kilrog's shoulder, high above us.

The monster raised its remaining hand and pointed at him; a thin ray of blackness shot out into Loras. Even from here, I could feel the cold despair of the horrible spell—one of the most evil in existence.

He screamed and fell as his body was covered in a black veil; he was dead.

The *Finger of Death* was a powerful necromantic spell that the nightwalker could only use once a day, but it had done its damage. Loras lay unmoving.

The last of the insects were popping out of me, and I struggled to my feet. My blood was leaking everywhere, along with that foul-smelling pus. I felt so tired … *if I could just lie down and rest for a bit …*

I snapped my head up. Unconsciousness was at the

door, but I had to finish. I couldn't let this evil man, this wicked *thing*, continue unchecked.

Clestus and it were engaged in an epic spell battle, once more. It was shooting Chain Lightning into both Clestus and Roland, while Clestus was firing his own *Magic Missiles* into Kilrog.

Both of them were still standing, although they were clearly injured. They were the last two of us standing.

Until now, anyway. Entirely on my feet, I started to walk forward.

Clestus saw me and cast something on Roland's axe.

Roland ran forward and hit Kilrog in the leg. Seeing its chance, it swiped him with its claw.

Luckily, he had spun, and the shield on his back met it, as he was flung several meters.

As Roland got to his feet, I saw Clestus fall from the monster's never-ending lightning attack. His body lay still and smoking.

I charged.

Kilrog saw me and tried to move, but his leg betrayed him. Clestus had imbued *Partial Petrification* onto Roland's axe.

Once again, Kilrog waited with open arms as I charged into him, jumping to hit his midsection.

As my horn buried into him, I felt the incredible force of his arms embracing me. Unable to breathe, I felt my life force being drained.

Finally, I was able to sleep ...

* * *

ROLAND

I KNEW whatever Clesus had cast on my massive double-sided battleaxe was bad news for the night-walker. Rushing forward, I struck it as high in its massive leg as I could. It swiped at me, but I had expected that. Spinning, I let it hit the shield that was still fastened on my back.

The force of the blow was incredible as I was flung onto the ground face forward and then rolling.

As I came to a stop, I stood. My wind had been knocked out of me, but I forced air back into my lungs.

Argent was charging it, and Clestus lay, smoking, on the ground.

I saw it bear hug her as she jumped and impaled the creature in the midsection. The two of them fell to the ground, embroiled in one another. The embrace looked almost tender, except for the nightwalker's crushing power and life-draining effect. The monster looked smug, as Argent was unconscious and surely dying.

Its vicious eyes were still amused as I cleaved Drek's mighty axe clean through its neck. The eyes, now vacant, spun away with its severed head. I watched the head bounce, then roll out of the opening in the outer wall, and begin its long fall to the ground.

I stood alone.

The battle was over.

PART IV

EPILOGUE

CHAPTER 8

DARK WIZARD KILROG

Kilrog awoke to a strange sensation.

As his eyes cracked open, he realized he was alive!

How?

The first thing he noticed was the awful smell—brimstone and sulfur. What he saw next made his breathing stop and his body freeze. Standing only a few meters away was an impossibly black warhorse. Her silver eyes were boring into his.

He was looking up at her from far below, which was weird. When he looked down, he saw his body was blubbery and hairless. His skin was pale white with sickly blue splotches. In horror, he reached up and felt a slack mouth with lots of tiny, sharp teeth.

Reeling mentally, he realized what he was—a *Dretch*.

One of the lowest minions of hell. Servants of greater demons. He knew who his master now was …

Where he was was just as terrifying—this must be one of the Planes of Hell, for that is where nightmares came from. And their queen now looked down at him. He knew he could not speak; the dretch had no such abilities. They could only communicate telepathically.

Welcome to Hell, Kilrog.

Onyx was enjoying the moment, he could tell.

Why am I still in your service, Onyx? I thought I would be banished to the lower planes to live in torment for eternity after abandoning you.

I could feel her amusement as she strode closer to look down upon me.

You are still quite useful to me, Kilrog. Besides, I am chaotic evil, not lawful evil. Your disregard for my well-being is actually quite amusing to me. However, as you clearly cannot be trusted either, I have gifted you a more ... easily destroyed body.

Don't worry. As you prove yourself to me anew, you will be rewarded again. But you have much to prove.

I lowered my head. Although I still possessed great magical ability, I had no gear: no weapons, no *power-stones*, no armor. I was utterly at her mercy, and we both knew it.

Yes, my master.

Hmm ... That's more like it ...

Since we have an eternity to get to know each other, let's plan for our eventual return to the Material Plane. It galls me to have been defeated by humans, but I am enraged it was by a ... a unicorn.

She said **unicorn** with a malice that was frightening —even to me.

We will avenge ourselves upon her, my lord, Onyx. The time will come.

Yes, my loyal servant. It will indeed ...

* * *

ARGENT THE UNICORN

MY EYES CAME OPEN, and I saw Roland standing above me. He had used *Potions of Healing* and some items from Clestus to heal me. Far from okay, but now awake, I stood.

Thank you, Roland. How is everyone else?

Roland looked at me a moment, realizing I was talking to him telepathically. He just spoke aloud, though.

"Blaine and Loras are dead, Clestus and Grace are unconscious, and Shivalt is just standing around being useless," he said

Then he chuckled.

I looked over and, sure enough, Shivalt was standing where I last saw him, completely immobilized. We were only being glib because we knew the *Total Paralysis* spell would wear off soon, and he would be alright.

I walked over to Grace and Clestus and cried unicorn tears on them. I wanted to do more, but I was too fatigued.

Thank you, Roland. You saved us.

"It was my honor, Argent," he replied.

A bodak had slain Blaine, and he would become one; there was nothing we could do except to cut off his head so he wouldn't.

Loras was lying on the ground. He looked peaceful, as though asleep—a sleep he would never return from.

I tried crying on them both, but I knew it was to no avail.

FLASH

Now, as a person again, I helped the others with healing spells.

Once we were all healed up again, we kept watch for the rest of the night, taking turns sleeping until sunrise. One of us was always stationed to release the boulder down the stairs, in case the keep's guards decided to attack us.

As the first rays of light cast their hue on the horizon, I used my innate *Beast Summoning* and waited.

Soon, an eagle arrived, and I was able to cast *Beast Speech* on it. Then I tied a note to its leg and instructed it to fly to Minoras Castle and deliver it to the Prince.

It looked majestic as it flew off into the morning sun.

I looked down and saw that all of the keep's guards had left. The hobgoblins and bugbears had long since looted what they could and left before the Prince's soldiers could arrive.

I am sure the head of the nightwalker spurred them on.

We ate, drank, and then camped another night, waiting for the Prince's forces to arrive.

* * *

THE NEXT MORNING, once everyone was awake, we kept watch for the Prince's forces.

Although the Prince would claim it as his keep, the items in it that we could carry were ours, as loot and spoils for our adventure. We would also bring the bodies of our fallen, along with extra spoils of war. After dispersing our found magic items, gems, jewelry, and coins, we would leave the rest of it for the soldiers to carry away for the benefit of Greenlove Village and the next of kin of their fallen. The rest was to be the profit of the realm. The Prince's soldiers would later give the rest of the town's share to them.

Kilrog's Keep itself was about to become part of the Minoras realm, as we heard a rumbling in the distance.

Looking down from the spire's openings, we saw that an entire battalion had shown up. Apparently, my warning of an ancient and angry black dragon's lair being here garnered an overwhelming response.

We headed down to meet the arriving army.

* * *

WAVING down to them from the battlements, we opened the portcullis and let them in. Scores of soldiers came inside the courtyard, and their leader approached us.

"Hail, adventurers, I am Commander Caligard of Prince Evan's army," the leader said. He was a big man and wore the shiny rank of a noble.

Clestus approached him.

"Mayor of Greenlove, with the party that avenged our village's attackers. We are thankful for your response, noble sir."

Commander Caligard nodded.

After all the introductions and explaining our story, the Commander assigned an entire platoon to help us recover our fallen, both here and at the ruins, and to bring back treasure for the town.

"I'm sure you understand that the realm will take its share and return to your town with the rest of your share?" he said.

"Aye, my liege, we understand," Clestus said.

All the soldiers who traveled with us back to Greenlove Village rode horses, and they kindly provided us with one each. We stopped at the ruins to retrieve the bodies of Drek and the other fallen soldiers. On the way back, we only encountered a few monsters, and when we did, the forty or so of us quickly handled them. The monsters with any intelligence did not engage us.

As we arrived in Greenlove, we delivered the news of the lost soldiers and laid Drek and the other soldiers to rest. His body would be taken to the Catacombs of the Dwarves, where he would lie in eternal rest, remembered as a Hero of Greenlove.

Joining the others, we all assembled for the memorial. Mayor Clestus, now in his elegant town mayor's robes, gave the eulogy. When he was done, he read the names of each of the ten soldiers and party members we had lost. Then he added the names of the three townsfolk that Onyx and Kilrog had killed at the pub. One of the injured from Kilrog's Chain Lightning also died from their wounds.

As the eulogy ended, Grace was quietly crying, and I did not move to wipe away the tears that fell from my eyes.

Now that the service for all of the fallen was over, we once again got ready to go our separate ways.

"Argent, will you please come visit us more?" Grace asked.

I could see the pleading in her eyes as she looked into mine.

"I will, I promise."

She nodded and then buried her head into Shivalt's shoulder. He lovingly stroked her hair.

"Goodbye. Perhaps I should instead say 'until we meet again,'" he said.

Nodding, I shook his outstretched hand, then, changing my mind, hugged them both. No more words were needed.

Thinking of this town that had become *my* town, my home outside of Hallowdale Forest, I turned and walked away. Through the familiar gate and across the meadow, I walked.

Would evil ever rest?

I knew, deep inside, it would not.

Today, though, the sun was shining brightly, and everything was in full bloom. I could smell the summer scents, and the birds, animals, and insects all went about their lives with no thought to the tribulations of humankind. As I entered the forest, I could see the withered plants already starting to heal and show vitality.

FLASH

As I changed into a unicorn, I trotted through my forest. The warm sunlight filtered down through the tree branches, and the melodies of beautiful songbirds welcomed me.

It was good to be home again.

ACKNOWLEDGMENTS

I want to thank you, first and foremost, my reader.

Without your support, creative authors and new books would not exist. Your enthusiasm is contagious to us, making us want to write amazing stories for you! Thank you again for spreading the word about our books, leaving us reviews, and purchasing our books.

Also, to my beta readers and editors, thank you.

I also want to thank, once again, an unusual group: roleplayers. Without the experience of these games in my youth, such as Dungeons & Dragons and GURPS, I would have been unable to bring this world's adventures to life so vividly.

ABOUT THE AUTHOR

RK Jack is a retired government agent with over thirty years of experience in federal law enforcement and the military, including many years as an instructor. With a background in martial arts, including the use of melee weapons, he enjoys portraying adventurers as real people and professional adventurers. He has always been interested in both teaching and sharing stories, which has lead to his new career as an author.

Now, an award-winning nonfiction and fiction writer, he mainly writes horror and dark fantasy adventures. It turns out that the same terrible monsters that haunt the fantasy world are even more prevalent—and equally horrifying—as those that appear in modern settings.

He looks forward to creating more stories and is always eager to hear new ideas from his fans.

CONNECT WITH THE AUTHOR

I hope you enjoyed this book!

As always, I would greatly appreciate it if you would leave an honest review for this book and/or other books by RK Jack. Your opinion matters a lot!

This is the second book in the Argent the Unicorn trilogy, with the final, thrilling installment already being written ...

I currently live in Denver, Colorado, and would be happy to visit your book club or group upon request. You can reach me anytime through my website: rkjackauthor.com.

Authors everywhere depend on you for them to continue writing their books. So ...

Thank you for your support!

9 7989 9005 6886